E.S.S. ENTERPRISE

Contents

Contents 1

INTRODUCTION 1

PROLOGUE 5

ACT ONE 1

    Chapter One – Earth Space Ship Enterprise 3

    Chapter Two – Transfer of Command 15

    Chapter Three – Incoming Storm 21

    Chapter Four – Shield Tests 31

    Chapter Five – Solar Emergency 37

ACT TWO 55

    Chapter Six – Where are we? 57

    Chapter Seven – Report 67

    Chapter Eight – Repairs and Realisation 75

    Chapter Nine – Making Plans 85

    Chapter Ten – Diagnosis Terrible 93

    Chapter Eleven – Commanders Meeting 103

    Chapter Twelve – Realisation 113

Chapter Thirteen – Two become One 119

Chapter Fourteen – It's a Wrap 129

Chapter Fifteen – Decent in the New Ranks...137

Chapter Sixteen – Captain's Orders..................145

ACT THREE..151

Chapter Seventeen – What the...........................153

Chapter Eighteen – You're the Man!.................157

Chapter Nineteen – How Bad? 165

Chapter Twenty – That Bad.................................175

Chapter Twenty-One – The New Road Home 187

Chapter Twenty-Two – Final Transfers 205

Chapter Twenty-Three – The Final Goodbye 211

Chapter Twenty-Four – A New Beginning 219

EPILOGUE ....a

GLOSSARY...g

INTRODUCTION

Like many people who follow space sciences with any enthusiasm, I think we have all wished that we could make some of our ideas, propositions and fantasies into reality. Many years ago I wondered if you could actually turn my favourite fictional spaceship, Star Trek's USS Enterprise, into something of a reality. While warp drive was a bit beyond me then, the one idea that got stuck in my head was the idea of a rotating wheel. The same design that has inspired writers and scientists for over a century, I thought that maybe you could put that wheel inside the main circular hull. At the time I had no understanding how a rotating wheel worked, or even its technical name.

Then I found what has become a great resource for many people, Wikipedia. Now I've been to university too, so I know not to rely upon it. But Wikipedia provides an incredible resource for exploring knowledge. Plus, given it is in essence a peer reviewed website, the science and math you find there is pretty accurate.

Through Wikipedia, I found out about the Rotating Wheel concept, that centrifugal force and inertia provide that so called gravity that keeps water in a bucket when you spin your arm around, and the many wonderful concepts that utilise this artificial gravity.

From Werner von Braun and Willy Lee's concept to reach Mars, to the Stanford Torus and the O'Neill Cylinder, the Rotating Wheel concept has been favoured by many.

Then around the summer of 2009 I conducted a thought experiment. How could we make a rotating wheel space station with our current technology?

There was going to be no problem getting most of such a station into space, however the problem of the "Ring" began to elude me. How to you lift up such a curved section into space when it is inherently not aerodynamic? One could encapsulate such a shape within a cylinder, even a shuttle, but that seemed like a waste of space.

Then it dawned upon me. Why not just send up a straight cylinder, but offset it with a wedge component? Or even better, incorporate said wedge into the actual shape of the cylinder. Like any object being launched into space, it would still need an aerodynamic 'tip', but that's how we send up satellites now.

Then the plan began to fall into place. Utilise rockets instead of shuttles to reduce the cost of launch and increase the frequency of launches, and instead of requiring a new crew to be sent to install each module make each module to a common design and have the initial station crews be a construction crew. So was born what I termed Space Station One.

Several of the technical aspects were still beyond me, such as rotating the wheel, but it quickly became apparent that with only a simple modification the design could not only be used for a space station, but also a space ship. By adding a module with fuel supplies and engines to a bottom of the station the concept become a ship.

Over the years I've been able to refine a lot of the design, gain more technical knowledge and solve some of the problems. I hope into the future I will be able to work with industry to help create such a station. As I have hinted in this book, I believe artificial gravity must be our next great technological achievement in space exploration. While it would most likely take more than a decade for us to know if centrifugal type gravity can adequate replace earth's gravity and alleviate some of the conditions associated with weightlessness, it is an endeavour we must undertake because in the words of many before me, "This Will Change Everything".

While you only see a glimpse of what such a station would look like, this book is about a ship to take on that design.

By basing the story in the near decades not to far from today I hope I've bought a sense of reality to the story as well as provide a guide on how a rotating wheel can be bought to reality.

And yes, she is named after that starship.

Nic Rankin

PROLOGUE

E.S.S. ENTERPRISE PRE-FLIGHT MEDIA BRIEFING
JOHN F. KENNEDY SPACE CENTER
MERRITT ISLAND, FLORIDA, UNITED STATES
08:00 E.S.T. JUNE 22, 2044

A large group of reporters have assembled at the John F. Kennedy Space Center in Florida, United States. The reporters begin taking their seats as a group of people enters the conference room, taking their seats at their various positions both behind the table and beside it.

"I'd like to thank everyone for coming today to the pre-flight media briefing for mission EX-08. I'm NASA Communications Director Nicole Sanderson. I'll let everyone introduce themselves."

"I'm Peter Knight, Kennedy Launch Director for this mission."

"I'm Mark Bridges, Earth Space Centre Deputy Chief Director."

"I'm Michael Foley, Commanding Officer of the Earth Space Ship Enterprise Shakedown Crew."

"Joining us today is also the rest of the Enterprise shakedown crew who will be available for a few questions at the end of this media briefing," informs Nicole, "Now before we get underway we want to update everyone on the International Space Station's Chief Engineer Richard Oliver. After a successful medical evacuation from the station he is now safe aboard the British Aircraft Carrier HMS Prince of Wales where he is receiving medical treatment. We still don't know what caused the Lieutenant to blackout but he is awake and aware and in good spirits. A separate briefing will be held later today to update you further on his condition.

"Now, we will go over launch preparations and countdown, then onto crew preparation then the quick Q and A and finally a few minutes for photos with the crew. Over to you Peter," continues Nicole.

"Thank You Nicole. I'd like to extend a warm welcome to the media gallery for showing up today," says Peter, "I can now inform you that the final loading of cargo into the Excalibur space shuttle has been completed in line with our preparation timetable. Launching on this mission are several experimentation racks designed to test the limits of the racking systems on both the ZeroG platforms as well as on the gravity rings. Consumable supplies including oxygen, water and coolant fluid are also loaded as well as the final load of food supplies. The crews' personal affects have also been loaded and we are installing the crew seating inserts as we speak. Last nights test loading and unloading of oxygen supplies went off without a hitch and the shuttle has passed its penultimate inspections. Currently weather is looking good with a 10% change of bad weather but we don't expect that to be a problem. The launch time of 14:28 Eastern Standard Time on the 23rd of June is still on track with a launch window of 23 minutes. I'll pass you over to Mark for the crew prep briefing."

"Thanks Pete," says Mark, "The crew enjoyed their flights from Houston yesterday and spent this morning beginning preparations for the final crew check tonight. They will check that their seat inserts have been correctly installed and run a final ground systems check. If all passes then fuelling of the launch rocket will begin at 07:30 tomorrow morning and the shuttle will take on fuel at 10:40. Crew ingress will begin at 11:10 with the standard launch procedures to follow. Commander Foley did you want to add anything?"

"I'll just say that it's great to finally be here and we are all excited to be on the final countdown to this most important mission," say Foley, "We are looking forward to the final checkout this evening and can't wait to get this shakedown mission underway."

"Okay, so if there is nothing further to add we will open up for some questions," Nicole says pointing to a reporter in the galley.

"Tom Smith, CNN. Have any of the fuelling problems that have occurred on previous S37 missions occurred during testing?"

"Those fuelling problems were part of the older D series of the S37," says Peter "We've redesigned the coupling fitting on both the shuttle and service towers with additional relief valves and so far the pressure problems haven't effected the E series."

"Mary Grey, CBS News. With the addition of several experiment modules to the Enterprise will the mission still last 3 months or will more time be added to the mission for the newer modules to be installed and tested?"

"The additional experiment racks were loaded to add more sensors to test the ship during various phases of acceleration and deceleration. They will only require a few hours to install and we don't need them till after we have dropped the landing S.E.V. on the moon."

"Alex," Nicole points out over the crowded galley.

"Alex Dmitri, NTV. There were communication problem between the Russian modules and the antenna array. Have these been fixed yet or will those modules be communicating independently."

"I believe those problems will be fixed during the initial phases of flight," says Mark, "As the systems are internal to the ship they won't require any spacewalks. The Russian modules have powerful enough transmitters themselves so there won't be any interruptions before being connected to the main array."

"Lawrence Hamburg, BBC. How is the crew coping knowing that they will be the first humans to go beyond the moon and how are their families holding up?"

"We are really excited to get out there and test this ship out," says Foley, "We all know that we will be very far away from home but we will be close enough that if anything does go wrong it won't take long to get back. That's a great reassurance to family and friends of the crew, and coupled with only a very short communications delay some of the crew may even be able to tell their children bedtime stories at night."

"Is that what your planning on Commander?" enquires Lawrence.

"I'm sure that the communications channels will be quite busy throughout the mission... but I wouldn't rule it out," replies Foley with a smile.

"Zan He, CCTV. How does it feel to officially welcome China to the Earth Space Centre and what are your hopes for the future of Chinese space cooperation?"

"This is one of the most proud moments that we've had at E.S.C.," says Mark, "For many decades China has aspired to be an advanced member of the space community and it has only been in the past few years that they have joined the international space cooperative community. We welcomed the first Taikonaut aboard the International Space Station to help install the Chinese ZeroG module on Enterprise last year and the relationship has been positive ever since. We welcome Ensign Guang Li to the ESC community and look forward to many fruitful years to come."

"Andrew Kallis, S.A. Today. With such a diverse crew from so many backgrounds how is the crew getting along?"

"We've been going great," says Foley, "Ever since I left the space station four years ago we've been looking long and hard for the best people to not only work together but also live together. We have all become close friends over the past four years and be grow from each other strengths. Things will be just fine up there."

"Quinton Miller New York Times. With Lieutenant Oliver's return to earth will Lieutenant Kōno still hold the title of first female Chief Engineer or has that gone to Anna von Braun on the space station?"

"While Lieutenant von Braun is acting station chief engineer there has been no decision made as to if she will replace Lieutenant Oliver as the permanent chief engineer," says Mark, "So I'm confident that Lieutenant Kōno will still be the first female Chief Engineer."

"John Wells from Space.com. We've seen over the past

couple of months an increase in solar activity leading to some pretty intense solar flares. Is this going to be any problem for the Enterprise and could there be any harm from a direct hit from one of these flares?"

"Over the past several years we've been deploying technologies to help shield a space craft from any problems that may be caused by a solar flare or coronal mass ejection," informs Mark, "We've tested magnetic shield generations on both the international space station and on the shuttles and they have withstood a magnetic force of 1200 nano-Tesla in Earths upper atmosphere. We are sure that there won't be many problems out there for Enterprise and her crew."

"We also shouldn't forget that Enterprise has two other shielding systems," adds Foley, "The radiation sheaths will absorb and reflect a lot of radiation even from a CME and the large physical parabola shield at the front of the ship will also play a vital roll in protecting the Enterprise and its crew."

"And finally Mark Ruben," says Nicole.

"Mark Ruben The Australian. Commander Foley, you're about to embark on one of the most important missions that humanity has ever attempted… to fly away from Earth on the first rotating wheel spaceship. How does it feel to be part of the crew achieving such an accomplishment?"

"While our mission will involve some routine tasks like heading out to the Lunar Observatory and dropping of a Landing Module it will also achieve some incredible achievements. The first human space flight to the L2 and L4 Lagrangian points are going to be the crowing achievements of this flight. But that will pail in comparison for where this ship was designed to fly, Mars, Titan, and beyond. Our shakedown journey will be important but also small in the story that will unfold before this ship. Enterprise was built to be a leader for humanity in space and I have a feeling she will perform that duty quite well and get us home safely ready for the real explorers to take her out into the final frontier."

"Okay people that concludes the question and answer part of todays briefing. I'll ask the crew of the E.S.S. Enterprise to stand together for photographs," says Nicole, "A reminder there will be one final photo opportunity at the crew assembly area outside the V.A.B. before the crew depart for the shuttle for their mission. That concludes todays briefing."

As the officials leave there seats Commander Michael Foley joins the rest of his crew standing for official photographs in front of the press galley. Behind all the smiles Foley is sure the rest of his crew is just as nervous as he is, heading into space in just over 27 hours for the mission of their lifetimes.

ACT ONE

Chapter One – Earth Space Ship Enterprise

Earth, graceful and elegant.

At more than 6000 kilometres in diameter and 24000 kilometres circumference it is the largest 'solid' planet in the Solar System. The Pacific Ocean is the largest body of water on the planet; spotted with tiny islands it's also one of the most uninhabited places on the planet after Antarctica. However the Pacific Ocean is the most important in its role as a 'radiator' of heat out of the Earth's oceans, leading to a high occurrence of severe weather events including hurricanes, typhoons and cyclones. It is also the most tectonically active with its massive underwater 'ring of fire', which impacts four of the planets seven continents. Earth is also the only planet that has developed complex and intelligent life. Despite being more than 4 billion years old, the human civilisation has developed only in the past 12000 years. In that time humanity has gone from just another animal struggling for survival with all other life to forging tools, utilising elements, creating societies and discovering science. The pinnacle of that scientific discovery is the exploration of space. Reaching space, orbiting the planet and travelling to another planetary body have all been crowning achievements. However it wasn't until the creation of artificial gravity in the late 2020's that the next achievement could be attempted.

In the distance, the Baja California peninsula can be seen unravelling slowly from the horizon. That's if 1000 kilometres per hour can be considered slow. In the far distance a speck of light can be seen above the curvature of the horizon.

"Excalibur to Houston, we have the complex in sight," says the voice of a female space shuttle pilot over a radio link.

"Copy Excalibur. We'll start from page 8, Paragraph 23," replies Mission Control in Houston.

"Page 8, 23," responds the pilot.

The Excalibur was by no means the biggest spacecraft you'd seen, based on the old stalwart that had been the backbone of the international space fleet, the S37-E. Derived from the secretive X-37 series of space planes, the S37 ushered in a new era of utility and flexible space flight. The first civilian S37-D was a scaled up variant of the X37 that could be used for variable missions. As an automated craft the S37-D flew cargo delivery missions to the first International Space Station, could be fitted with 'Robonauts' to fix satellites and even had a passenger pod capable of sending up to 16 passengers into space.

As humanities space exploration appetite grew to a new golden age so came the need for a craft that could survive longer duration missions. The extended S37-E was built bigger and longer to not only survive the harshness of space beyond the protection of Earth, but to carry enough fuel to get us back from where we were going.

In the distance, the speck of light began to take shape. Looking like a cross suspended in the heavens the second International Space Station, or ISS2 as it had became to be known, began to emerge from the shadow of Earth. ISS2 had been the pinnacle of space engineering. Not only did it inherit some of the younger modules of its original namesake, it was humanities first attempt to create the one comfort of home that space travel lacked. Gravity.

Upon closer inspection the horizontal arm of the station was no arm, but a spinning wheel. Made up of 44 modules each was lifted into space not in the belly of a space plane, but atop a rocket just like a satellite. Each of these 20 metre straight cylinders has a wedge on each end. With each wedge tipping the next cylinder 9 degrees, a ring is created with a continuing circumference of more than 800 metres. Connected to the central Core by two 140 metre arms the ring rotates at around two and a half revolutions per minute, creating the sensation of gravity through inertia and centrifugal force. Such an achievement was considered the next big technological achievement of humanities space travels. With artificial gravity, all problems of weightlessness in space are eliminated. ISS2 provided our first experimental platform for artificial gravity as we would need to use it in space, while previous attempts had been limited in both volume and utility. ISS2 allows humanity to not only continue the spirit of cooperation of its predecessor, but to conduct experiments to find out if this type of gravity would be beneficial to us. While the sensation feels a bit different, biological and medical problems such as bone density deterioration and heart issues are addressed removing the one major limitation that we had to space habitation and exploration, Time.

The Core of the station was split into two sections, fore and aft. Referring to sections above and below the ring respectively, the fore section contains an airlock, the engineering sections and the truss segment containing many of the exterior equipment like radiators and the solar arrays. Moving down to the aft section of the Core, the living quarters contains the sleeping berths and personal storage and cooking equipment. The next modules are what have come to be called the ZeroG modules pointing out from the core in a cross. These are varying experiment modules that each national contributor has created and sent up containing a variety of equipment and experiment modules. Below is the primary docking module capable of holding five craft at a time, though many nations also use their ZeroG modules for docking of both personnel and cargo craft.

With all its technological achievements, the most amazing fact of ISS2 is its construction cost.

While its predecessor cost upward of $130 billion United States dollars, this station cost only $100 billion. Not only overcoming the construction expense of the original ISS, but also utilising a new common modular standard for the construction of all the stations modules helped achieved this. By making all modules to a common standard, the costs associated with making each module to different specifications were eliminated. This still allowed for customisation of the systems installed on each module by using the common space racking standard that had been used for decades, but by having a common chassis and design many costs can be consolidated. With each module being a straight cylinder, each of the station modules was lifted into space not in the belly of a space shuttle but atop a simple rocket. Considered the biggest cost component of the original ISS, by cutting the cost of launch by more than

60% and by making the first crews of the new station construction crews the massive construction costs of its predecessor were reduced greatly. By having that crew conduct the installation of new arriving modules, each could be sent up with only a two-week gap from the last. This lead to ISS2 being constructed in less than 4 years completed in 2029. Over the next 15 years various 'habitat' expeditions were made to the station to find out if humans could survive long-term duration in what has become to be known as 'centro' gravity. Initial experiments lasted only weeks, but the last habitat expedition crew spent more than 4 years on the Ring of ISS2. This was the longest test of endurance that any space flight had undertaken, and that crew passed with flying colours.

However ISS2 isn't the destination for Excalibur. As she approaches the station a startling site emerges from the shadows.

A Twin.

Not completely identical though just as impressive.

Humanities first interplanetary spaceship, Earth Space Ship Enterprise, makes her majesty felt. While sporting the same basic features from her space station cousin, the Enterprise has several unique features. At the very "bottom" of the ship, where spacecraft would usually dock on the station, are several huge engines. These new Helicon Double Layer Thruster engines are more than capable of thrusting the Enterprise to escape velocity of any planet in the solar system. The engines use a magnetic field to guide and hold the gas plasma reaction from the engine. As the magnetic field begins to deteriorate beyond its source it creates a magnetic 'nozzle', reducing the need to use a strong and tough metal. Further up the central Core are the fuel pods containing the engines primary fuel Argon and Hydrogen. Beyond the fuel pods is the primary truss containing the solar arrays. Above the primary truss are a couple of storage modules, which lead to the Interchange module and arms leading out to the Ring.

Above the Interchange module are some additional storage modules leading to the ships ZeroG platform. Currently there are either one or two modules attached to the four ports on the ZeroG platform. Above the ZeroG platform are the docking ports for the various spacecraft including capsules and the Space Exploration Vehicle. At the very "top" of the Enterprise is a flexible carbon fibre shield. Once unfurled, this imposing parabola is designed to reflect and cushion any space debris that may find its way toward the Enterprises Core Section. New radiation shielding technologies allow the exterior of the ship to be draped in a protective fabric, providing an easy to replace exterior shield that is as simple as rolling away a rug when ready for disposal. Not only does this shield protect from radiation, it also acts as protection for the Ring modules as the parabola doesn't quite span the entire diameter of the Ring.

It is this ship that will fulfil the next great space exploration achievement, visiting another planetary body.

Once the 'Habitat' expeditions were completed on ISS2, it was clear to all participants that Enterprise should be constructed. Even after the first 2 year expedition authorities on Earth decided to delay missions to Mars using the S37-E and concentrate on this ship as their best option. Being able to send more than 100 crewmembers and up to 8 landers, plus the extra time the 'centro' gravity from the Ring affords a mission to another planet, it was clear their minds were made up.

As the Excalibur approaches a docking port on Enterprise, it retracts its solar array. Unlike normal, the docking process isn't entirely automated. With the US ZeroG module 'Intrepid' having only just been installed, the Automated Docking System hasn't been activated yet.

Shuttle Pilot Lieutenant Helen Foster has been given the task of a manual docking. Moving at rate of only 5 centimetres per second in the final stage sets a slow pace only the most patient astronauts qualify for.

"Extend Berthing Module," Lieutenant Foster commands over her radio.

About 5 meters away the docking port extends out about 50 centimetres from the Enterprise hull while the same occurs on the Intrepid module.

"BM Extended, ready for final alignment," comes the reply from the Enterprise.

"Beginning Final Alignment," radios Foster as she activates a laser sight system. Normally, the computers on both sides of the berthing modules would talk with each other and make the final adjustments. However Lieutenant Foster must make the tricky judgment for herself. She must align six sets of teeth into groves on the Enterprise. A camera system relays the image of three mirrors. Once each of these three mirrors shows the alignment lasers, it indicates the Excalibur is on the correct pitch, roll and yaw. Once the berthing modules are aligned, Foster glides Excalibur toward Enterprise. With only the finest of grinds, the modules capture each other. Excalibur activates its magnetic 'soft latch', causing the Enterprise to mechanically move its 'hard latches' into place.

"Soft and hard latch confirmed. Begin 90 seconds no ops," Enterprise radios.

90 Seconds of no ops is designed to detect if any unusual anomalies have occurred from docking by detecting any abnormal vibrations or sensor readings.

"No Ops complete and cleared," Enterprise announces, "Welcome to the Enterprise."

With a hiss and whirl, the docking hatch of the Excalibur opens. Once secured, each of the passengers begin to float through the hatches. First through the hatch is the most important person of the mission.

"Commander Foley, welcome aboard the Enterprise."

"Thank you Lieutenant Harrison," the Commander exclaims. A fit male in his mid forties, Commander Mike Foley is a 20 year space veteran. Having conducted his now eighth space flight, Foley was the most experienced astronaut either on or off the planet. Having served on the original ISS, tagging along to the moon in the Orion and served two expeditions on ISS2 made Foley almost too qualified for the mission.

"May I introduce to you my first officer Lieutenant Commander Jessica Ross."

Jessica Ross is one of the "stars" of the NASA. Serving on both Orion and ISS2 made her a great candidate for the position. Even though she had been overlooked for the first officer position with Enterprise's first operational crew, NASA didn't want their prime candidate ruled out entirely. Who knows, Ross may even be the commanding officer of a future Enterprise mission. But for the moment, she settles for First Officer of the shakedown crew.

One by one, crewmembers transferred from Excalibur onto Enterprise and are quickly dispatched to their sections for their initial briefing and orientation. Sixteen crew in total, it is these men and women who will be conducting the shakedown mission for the ship.

"Commander Fisher is in Ops and requested to see you as soon as you came on board," Harrison informs Foley.

"Would you like to join us Lieutenant?" Foley offers.

"Not this time sir, but we will catch-up before you depart," Harrison smiles as he turns toward the transport pod strung between the station and Enterprise.

"Last I remember you owe me a drink Lieutenant."

"Last I remember you cheated... sir!" Harrison replies, with a hint of sarcasm.

"Perhaps a rematch then?" Foley offered with a grin.

"Last time I checked there were no pool tables in space," Harrison replies as he closes the transport pod airlock and departs for the ISS2.

Commander Foley then pushes off with ease floating up the Core of the ship.

Why can't moving around on Earth be this simple? Foley thinks.

While not exactly an art to master Foley couldn't help but notice the mission rookies still struggling with movement in space, still trying to 'Walk' their way around their orientation. While lending a hand loading equipment into some racks, parts of the Enterprise interior still look like a construction zone. With Excalibur making the penultimate delivery of equipment, it is Commander Foley's crew who will make final installations with the help of the ISS crew. They will then conduct the shakedown of the ship, heading out to the moon to test the landing SEV and then accelerating forward out of Earths orbit before swinging back to the moon to pick up the landing SEV then back to the station. While not heading out to a neighbouring planet, it will be the furthest humanity has ventured from Earth since the now regular missions to the moon.

Foley makes quick time to the Interchange Module. Here the Core narrows to a small 1 metre diameter pipe keeping both the upper and lower sections of the Core connected while the Ring rotates beyond. Access to the Interchange Module is through one of two portholes either side of the narrowed Core module. Once through the portholes the interchange module rotates freely with two elevators opposite each other. These elevators are entered from the top in the interchange module while the occupants exit through a door on the side of the elevator once it reaches the Ring. Each elevator has two decks mirroring the layout of the Ring modules with the lower deck dedicated to cargo storage while the upper deck is split in half with two passenger seats on one side and more cargo storage on the other. Several of the station and Enterprise crew members have already loaded both the upper and lower decks on one of the transport elevators with cargo ready to send down to the Ring.

Lieutenant First Class John Crane, one of the station engineers assigned to test the science systems is placing a final container into the elevators storage section, "That should do it sir, she's ready to head down when you are."

"Thanks Lieutenant," Foley replies as he floats over to a console tapping the intercom, "Commander Ross report to the Interchange Module."

"I'm surprised that they didn't choose Commander Ross for this ships first mission," Crane exclaims.

"I happen to think she's one of the best," Foley replies, "but for some reason she requested this assignment."

"A career move perhaps?" Carne questions.

"Maybe, it could set her up to be the CO on a future mission," reasons Foley.

"Well, it seems Commander Fisher wants me to head over to the station. They are having some troubles with an infra-red sensor and want me to take a look at it," Crane informs the Commander.

"Better get to it. I want everyone here at 0600 hours for our first mission briefing."

Chapter Two – Transfer of Command

While the trip down the arm that connects the Core to the Ring is a short 140 meters, the journey takes about 10 minutes. The elevator can move faster, but the slow trip allows the occupants to adjust to the sensation of gravity just like they would during re-entry and landing on Earth.

"Oh, I forgot that feeling," Ross exclaimed.

"What's that, you didn't leave the oven on?" Foley joked.

"No," Ross chuckled, "Centro gravity. It's been five years since my expedition on ISS2."

"It does feel different, more like a 'Push' instead of a 'Pull'."

"How long was it since your ISS2 expedition sir?" Ross asks

"Just under four years, though watching the docking from the shuttle bought it all back to me," Foley replies as he browses over mission orders.

Just like every elevator on Earth, a chime plays and the motion slows to a stop. As the occupants rise from their seats the door opens presenting Commander Fisher and an Ensign.

"Commander Foley welcome to the Enterprise," Fisher offered with a grin.

"Edward, long time no see," Foley replies with a warm smile.

"Almost four years."

Commander Edward Fisher is the current ISS2 expedition leader. Fisher entered the British Space Service after the European Union began recruiting more astronauts for the extended mission of the original ISS. Both Commanders are veterans of their respected agencies.

"Too long," Foley replies, "and this is my First Officer Lieutenant Commander Jessica Ross"

"I've heard nothing but great things about you commander," Fisher offers.

"I'm sure I'll be hearing great things about you during this shakedown Commander," Ross responds.

"As long as you don't hear the not-so-great things I'll be happy," Fisher replies giving Foley a sideways glance, "So, are the two of you up for a stroll around the Ring?"

"I'll stay and help of load the cargo Commander," Ross offers too Foley, "Perhaps give you two a chance to catch up."

"Sounds good Ross," replies Foley.

Ross nods the two goodbye and heads down to the lower deck with the ensign to help unload the supplies and cargo. Much like ISS2, the Enterprise Ring modules are split into two decks. With a diameter of 6 meters, two decks around 2.4 meters high are easily accommodated with enough space above the top deck and below the bottom deck to allow conduits and cabling. Moving in a forward rotation direction, beyond a storage module is one of the crew quarter's modules, each containing up to 20 rooms, of which two can be allocated to each crewmember. Next is an emergency shelter module built with thicker walls, the module also contains not only the fresh water and food supplies, but also has two escape pods. Each pod, based on a space capsule can hold up to 8 people and can join together. While this design works on ISS2, with the isolated nature of the Enterprises missions the entire module has been designed to jettison. Four of these Emergency Shelter modules on the Ring coupled with the Escape Pods attached to the sides of the Core should provide a stricken crew with enough supplies and engine power to meet up with a rescue craft. Prior to Operations is an Offices module, containing 8 rooms that can be used for a variety of purposes. Each room contains direct data links to the computer cores and communications systems.

"New car smell," Foley smirks.

"You'd think with all the clean rooms and decontamination they would get rid of that smell," Fisher says, "but with the final set of air filters Excalibur just bought up and the fact you guys will be living here it won't last long."

"Oh come on Commander, we have to leave something for the first crew when they get up here," Foley says, "So, how is she holding up?"

"All systems are operating as they should, though we did have problems with one of the power transfer cables through the Core conduit bit that's been replaced," Fisher replies, "Rotation has also gone off without a hitch, even the transfer platforms are performing as expected."

Transfer platforms are special clamps that are designed to transfer equipment on the outside of the station from the Core to the Ring and back. Each clamp has two sets of wheels, which attach to a special rail system where the interchange module connects to the station. The rail allows the clamp to remain attached to one side while allowing it to pick up the speed of the interchange modules rotation, then transferring from one rail to another. This helps prevent any loss of momentum of the Ring.

"Are you expecting something to go wrong?" Foley enquires.

"You know what it's like with space programs. Something always goes wrong, you just hope it's before you set out on your mission," Fisher replies.

"That's what we're here for, we are the shakedown crew after all," says Foley, "We are the ones that will shake the bolts loose and crash the computers, all before the Enterprise even starts its first mission."

"It may as well be a first mission," Fisher exclaims, "A trip to the moon to land a expedition SEV, then on to L2, out to L4 then back to the moon to pick up the module then back to us."

"That's only going to be a small trip for this ship," Foley replies.

"Small Trip, you're going to be the first humans to leave the Earth planetary system. The furthest humans have ever been away from Earth is the far side of the moon. Even the shuttle you arrived on was designed to head out to Mars but they never quite sent it out there," Fisher says with a small hint of regret.

"I think command realised if we can simulate gravity that will have greater benefits then a loop out to the nearest planet and back," Foley responds, "That way we can stay out there for a few years instead of the shortest period of time. You don't want to go on holiday to the other side of the planet too have to get right back on the plane that day and go home."

"You're right, I just wish it was me heading out there," Fisher relents.

"At least you've got the protection of Earth's atmosphere,

out there all we've got is a carbon fibre shield and the walls beside us," Foley exclaims as they enter Operations.

Module R1 is the Operations module. Here the operations of the entire ship are monitored and commanded. One of only a few single deck modules the floor lowers to allow optimal usage of space. 'Ops' has 5 banks of computer consoles with seating for up to 15 personnel plus a small office on one end. In the centre of the deck is the proverbial Captains Chair facing 'forward' to a large display where a sixth set of consoles would otherwise be. Each bank of consoles can be programmed for various tasks, though usually are grouped into relates sections such as Operations, Navigation, Science.

At the far side of the module, an Alert sounds.

"A Priority One has arrived for you Commander," Lieutenant Jackson informs the Commanders from the Ops console.

"Yes Lieuten-" Both Commanders reply.

"I suppose you're still technically in command," Foley tells Fisher.

"Read it out Lieutenant," Fisher requests.

"Message from ISS Command Houston. Emergency Alert. Coronal Mass Ejection X7b detected at UTC 1635 June 24 heading to Earth. Expected impact at UTC 0900 June 25 with peak intensity of 1750 nT disruption at 1330 UTC June 25. Advise test and activation of magnetic shield generators on both craft by UTC 0600 June 25. Reorient the station and ship for a reduced orbit. Further instructions to follow."

"1750 nano-Telsa," Foley says.

"That's huge," Fisher says, "The Carrington event was

1600 nT."

"Are the Enterprises generators installed?" Foley asks.

"It's not the Enterprise I'm worried about," Fisher responds concerned "We had to take ours offline last week for refit."

"Will you be able to install it in time?" Foley enquires.

"If I can have a few of your engineers, we'll need to conduct a space walk."

"Certainly, give me an hour and we'll send some over once your crew are back on the station."

"Well then Commander, I hereby transfer the Enterprise into your possession and command," Fisher announces.

"I relieve you Commander," Foley replies.

"I am relieved," says Fisher.

"Note in ships log the transfer of command and notify Houston Lieutenant," Commander Foley orders.

"Aye Captain!" the Lieutenant replies.

Commander Fisher taps a ship intercom panel and orders "Fisher to ISS crew. Head back to station immediately."

Chapter Three – Incoming Storm

As ISS and Enterprise crewmembers swap positions in Ops, Captain Foley takes his seat, "Captain to Lieutenant Kōno, what is the status of the magnetic shield generators?"

"All 4 have been installed but only 3 tested Captain," Lieutenant Naomi Kōno replies.

"We need all four tested together and operating at full efficiency by 0600 tomorrow," Foley orders.

"Yes sir, any particular reason why?" Lieutenant Kōno asks.

"You're about to find out Lieutenant," Foley replies, "The station is going to need a couple of engineers sent over as soon as possible. I want them departing within the hour,"

"Yes sir."

The captain taps his intercom for a ship wide broadcast.

"This is the Captain. We've received an alert from command that an X7 coronal mass ejection has been detected heading toward Earth and is expected to arrive at around 0900. The CME has an expected peak intensity of 1750 nT on the magnetosphere. We will be activating our magnetic shield generators at 0600 and we are reorienting the ship to lower our orbit if necessary. Ensure that the ship is ready for this as the shields are only design to protect us from a hit of 1600 nT. We've got 12 hours to get the Enterprise ready. I know we can do it."

"The last transfer capsule with ISS crew has departed Captain," Lieutenant Shipway informs the Captain.

"Very good Lieutenant. Captain to Kōno, The final transit

capsule has left. Once they return I want our crew to head over."

"I've assigned Lieutenants Doria and Madison to head over; they will be ready in about 15 minutes," Kōno replies.

Lieutenant Naomi Kōno is the foremost expert in space engineering from Japan. She has spent seven years as an active JAXA astronaut including two trips to ISS2. Graduating from University of Tokyo's School of Engineering at age 22, Naomi Kōno spent two years working in the Japanese aerospace industry as part of the team that designed the central module connecting the Core to the Ring arms which gave her an invitation for JAXA entry. Kōno was selected for her rapport with NASA astronauts due to her training with them in the class of 2030. This is also the first time a Female has been selected as a mission chief engineer since the creation of the position with the ISS2.

In engineering Kōno begins the testing procedure for MSG Unit 3, the final generator yet to be fully tested.

"Ensign Smith, you've had intermediate gravity experience. Head to module A4 with a tool kit and monitor the generator from the elevator shaft," Kōno orders, "Engineering to Ops, we are going to shut down the Forward arm elevator to test the final shield generator. We will also be taking offline the water recyclers in the forward Core and shutting down the non essential systems in the ventral ZeroG modules."

"Understood," comes the reply from Ops.

"Lieutenant Diarra I want you to monitor the power flow to the generator," Kōno instructs "Ensign Paton, monitor the ships systems to ensure the power to the critical systems is uninterrupted."

"Yes Lieutenant," the Ensign replies.

"Lieutenant, prepare to divert power from the ventral ZeroG modules and shutdown the water recycling systems on the upper Core. That should provide us with enough power. We'll wait till we are ready to activate the generator prior to shutting down the modules," Kōno orders.

"Ops to Engineering, Lieutenants Doria and Madison have departed and the elevator on the forward arm is empty."

"Thank you, send the elevator to the Core side and release for manual control," Kōno requests.

"Ready to shut down the water recyclers Lieutenant," Lieutenant Diarra informs Kōno.

"Shut them down Lieutenant."

"Smith to Engineering, I've arrived at the Interchange module."

"Good Lieutenant. Once the elevator arrives head to the generator at the Core side of A2. It will be to the aft of the elevator," Kōno orders.

"Water recyclers offline," says Diarra.

"Good, standby to shut down the ZeroG modules."

"Smith to Engineering, I've arrived at the generator. All looks good for the test," Smith informs engineering.

"Don't forget to monitor the temperature of both the generator and the power couplings. They were getting a bit hot during the testing of the other generators," Replies Kōno.

"We're ready to shut down the ZeroG modules Lieutenant," says Diarra.

"O.k. I'll control the power flow into the generator. Shut

down the systems on the ZV2 module," Kōno orders.

"Shut down command sent," Diarra replies, "Power levels dropping to 70% normal."

"At 50% I'll power up the generators control computers," Kōno responds.

"Power levels at 50%," says Diarra.

"Powering up the computers," Kōno informs.

"Ships systems stable," the Ensign informs.

"The generators computers are online, setting for single operations mode," says Kōno.

"Module ZV2 is at 40% standby power," Diarra informs.

"That will do," Kōno says, "prepare to deactivate the systems on ZV1."

"Smith to Engineering, everything looks good here. The computers are operating within specifications."

"When we begin to charge the power capacitor, monitor the power coupling temperature," Kōno orders, "If it gets close to 70 degrees Celsius inform us."

"Will do," Smith replies.

"Begin the shut down sequence on ZV1," Kōno orders, "Inform me when it reaches standby."

"Yes Lieutenant, shutting down ZV1," Rawat replies, "Power levels dropping to 80%, 70%, 60%."

"Harrison, standby for capacitor charging," Kōno informs the Lieutenant.

"Power is at 40% standby," says Diarra.

"Beginning the charging sequence," Kōno informs.

"Power transfer stable, systems are normal," the Ensign informs.

"The capacitor is at 60%, 70%," says Kōno.

"Coupling temperature is at 60 degrees," Smith informs.

"Capacitor charge at 80, 90%, temperature reading?" Kōno orders.

"Temperature stabilising at 65 degrees," Smith replies.

"Capacitor is fully charged," Kōno informs, "Engineering to Ops, we are ready to activate the Magnetic Shield Generator. Shut down the non-essential systems on the forward section of the ring."

"Shutting them down now Lieutenant," the Captain replies.

"What is the temperature on the Capacitor?" Kōno requests.

"Capacitor temperature is within specifications," Smith replies.

"Non essential systems are offline engineering, ready for the test," the Captain informs.

"Generator ready," Diarra informs.

"Systems stable," says Paton.

"OK, activating MSG Unit 3 to 25%," says Kōno while tapping a button.

"Power flow stable, generator is at 25%," Diarra informs.

"Temperature stable," Smith communicates.

"Increasing to 60%, Ops standby on the detectors," Kōno orders.

"Detectors active," Ops replies.

"Generator is at 60%," says Diarra.

"Detecting a field reduction equivalent of 950 nT," Ops informs.

"That's within spec, how's she doing Smith," Kōno asks.

"All's well down here, the coupling is at 77 degrees."

"Let's push it up to 100%," says Kōno as she changes the

power settings.

"Detecting a field reduction equivalent of 1500 nT," Ops informs.

"Generator stable," Diarra informs.

"Systems stable," says Paton.

"That's close enough, shutting down the MSG," says Kōno, "We'll do the fine tuning when we conduct the combined systems test in a couple of hours."

"Generator is offline," informs Diarra.

The interior of the space station looks almost the same as that of the Enterprise. With the Enterprise being a derivative of the station, the only difference is the advancement of some technologies. The station still has cables and conduits snaking through each of the airlocks between modules and exposed racking while on the Enterprise they are all covered by panels. This is due to the continually changing nature of the station, while the Enterprise doesn't change its equipment outside of refits between assignments. The Enterprise also has warmer coloured panelling compared to the straight white of the station.

"von Braun to airlock, how are our team doing," Lieutenant Anna von Braun requests.

"Lieutenant Commander Singh and Ensign Coulton are about halfway through their acclimatisation sir," Lieutenant Parry responds.

"We need them out the airlock as soon as the generator unit is ready to send out," von Braun orders, "We're only going to be about an hour."

"They will need longer than that," Parry replies.

"Lieutenant, in four hours we are going to be hit by a coronal mass ejection bigger than the Carrington event. If that unit isn't installed in two hours we won't have time to test it and the station will be venerable," von Braun responds, "They need to be out there as soon as they are ready."

"We have re-assembled the generator Lieutenant," Ensign Doria informs von Braun, "We just need to vacuum decompress it to check the fittings are solid then we can send it out."

"How long will that take?" von Braun asks.

"Half an hour if everything's right, about an hour if we need to make any modifications," Doria responds.

"Take it to the vacuum chamber it the ZeroG lab and test it," von Braun orders.

Anna von Braun had a reputation to live up to. The great granddaughter of the famous rocket engineer Wernher von Braun, it wasn't until Anna undertook a study of her great grandfathers work did she even consider following in his footsteps. Once she graduated high school she attended Technische Universität München, graduating will full honours. After returning to the United States she was offered a position with a leading private space company to help design the new S37-E for deep space endurance. It wasn't until she returned to Germany to raise her family that being an astronaut became her career path. Anna trained alongside with ESA astronauts and was invited to take a position on the ISS2 following the death of the original station chief engineer.

"Houston to Station," the call radios in on the main communications channel.

"Fisher here," Commander Fisher responds.

"Station, we've got some bad news. It looks like the CME is coming in faster than expected. It will be here about 4 hours early. The L1 solar observatory is already beginning to experience the early effects. We will cut the spacewalk short when satellites in GEO begin to show any effects."

"Copy that Houston. Notify us when to end the walk," Fisher replies.

"Will do station, Houston out."

"Fisher to Parry, how much longer will the spacewalkers need to finalise the install of the generator," Fisher requests.

"They have only just reached the fixture commander," Parry replies, "It's going to take at least two hours to be installed."

"You might not have that long Lieutenant. We've got word the CME is going to arrive 4 hours early and command wants us to cut the walk short when satellites in geosynchronous orbit start to experience its effects," Fisher informs Parry.

"That means we've only got an hour max commander," Parry responds.

"Commander I'm here with Parry," von Braun interrupts, "If the team installs only the external connections they should finish in about an hour and we will be able to finalise the installation from inside the station."

"Instruct the team Lieutenant," Fisher orders.

"Sir, if the team don't make the correct connections outside we won't be able to correct them," von Braun warns, "Those space suit have nowhere near the protection that the station offers in the early stage of the CME impact."

"Understood Lieutenant, the team will have to do the best job they can," Fisher responds.

In engineering, von Braun begins a team briefing with the crew.

"This is going to be one of the most taxing operations we have ever needed to conduct on the station. We will need everyone to perform to their best. All the ZeroG modules will need to be put into standby and all non-essential systems in the Core shutdown. Ensure over the next couple of hours each modules batteries are fully charged encase of power interruptions and the circuit breakers are installed," von Braun informs, "Lieutenants Coulton and Oliveira I want you working on the Dorsal ZeroG Modules, Ensign Yang and Lieutenant Italy head too ZeroG Port, Ensign Watts and Lieutenant Crane to ZeroG Ventral, Lieutenant Nishizawa and Diarra over to ZeroG Starboard. Lieutenant Commander Ryan, if you can head up to the Truss with Lieutenant Volkoff and start down from there and assist the spacewalk team when they come back in that would be great. The remainder of you will be working down from engineering with me where we will meet up at the ZeroG modules and assist where necessary."

"Will the spacewalk team be assisting us?" Ryan enquires.

"As soon as they can if they are able. Keep them on 100%

oxygen if necessary," von Braun orders, "Any further questions?"

None of the team responds.

"Remember to keep the docking systems active on any attached craft as they may be needed in a last resort evacuation," von Braun reminds the team, "Let's get to it. Parry, provide the spacewalkers with assistance if needed."

"von Braun to Ops, I've dispatched the teams to begin powering down the stations systems."

"Thanks Lieutenant," Fisher responds.

"Commander, we are being hailed by Enterprise," Jackson informs the Fisher.

"Put it through," Fisher asks.

"Enterprise to Station," Foley says

"We hear you Enterprise," Fisher responds.

"In response to this CMS arriving early, we are going to test and calibrate our generators early in about 90 minutes at 0230. Does that sound fine with you guys?"

"Sure Captain, we're just starting to shut down our systems now and the installation team should be back in the station by then," Fisher responds, "But we're going to cut it close. If worse comes to worse, could we send a few crew over to the ship?"

"Of course Commander. Good luck," Foley responds, "Enterprise Out."

Chapter Four – Shield Tests

Two hours later, the Enterprise is conducting its final calibration test of the magnetic shield generators.

"Kōno to Diarra, adjust the resistance up to 320 ohms."

"Coupling adjusted," Diarra responds.

"Resonance is stabilising," Paton informs Kōno, "FRE is holding at 1580 nT on all detectors."

"Very good Ensign," Kōno says, "We will leave the generators active for a few more minutes. Kōno to Ops."

"Foley here."

"We have finished calibrating the MSGs and we will shut them down in a few minutes. You can inform the station they can begin their calibration once ours has deactivated," Kōno informs the Captain.

"Thank you Lieutenant." Foley responds.

On the bridge Foley contacts the station.

"Station here," Fisher responds.

"We have finished our calibration Commander. You can begin yours in a few minutes." Foley informs the station.

"I wish it was that easy," Fisher says, "We have almost completed the installation but it's going to cut it thin."

"Do you want to evacuate any of you crew over here?" asks Foley.

"They are all still shutting down our systems, the Core systems are on standby but we are having trouble with the Intrepid's docking system drawing too much power. We are trying to isolate the problem," Fisher responds, "We might need to seal the capsule hatch if we can't get it fixed soon."

"Good luck again," Foley replies.

"We seem to be using all of it up over here. Station out," Fisher closes.

"Foley to Kōno, the station is having a problem with the docking systems on one of their modules, contact Lieutenant von Braun and see if you can assist."

"Yes sir," Kōno replies, "We have now shutdown the magnetic shield generators. I advice we keep them on standby."

"Sounds good Lieutenant, Ops out," Foley responds, "Lieutenant Foster, how are the preparations going to realign for a lower orbit?"

"As soon as the station completes its spacewalk we will co-ordinate for a simultaneous rotation on the pitch of the station to place as little stress on the transit and communications cabling as possible," Foster replies.

While under construction, the ISS and Enterprise have had a variety of configurations. Initial components were docked to the station as any other module would be, but as the size and volume of the ship has grown to even outgrow the station both are now tethered to each other via four cables. Not only do these cables act as guide wires for the transport pods, they also provide a fibre communications and electrical link. However as each new component, from solar panels to communications arrays are installed on the Enterprise all but the transfer functions have now become redundant. The cable is installed on the upper half of the station near its solar panels and the lower half of the Enterprise where its solar panels shoot out in a cross from the core, unlike the station that has its panels in the truss above its Ring. At 200 metres in length there is more than enough room to accommodate the 80 metre long solar panels of the ship.

"Kōno to Ops, I recommend pulling the solar arrays by about 20 meters. We won't need their full generation capacity and the reduced volume needed to protect the ship will strengthen the magnetic shields."

"The reduced power isn't going to affect any of our other systems?" Foley enquires.

"No Captain, we are still on standby with non-essential systems offline we are only consuming about 40% of normal usage."

"Sounds like a plan Lieutenant, proceed when ready," says Foley.

"Commander, we've got an alert coming in from Houston. Outer constellation satellites in GEO are beginning to experience the effects of the CME. We will begin to experience the first effects of the CME in about 45 minutes," Lieutenant Jackson relays to Commander Fisher.

"Fisher to spacewalk team, your time is up. Start heading back to the airlock now," the Commander orders into his intercom.

"Singh here sir, we are almost there. We have only a few connectors to install then attach the outer casing," Lieutenant Commander Singh replies.

"von Braun, how long will that take?" Fisher asks.

"A couple of minutes for the cables, about ten for the casing," von Braun responds.

"Is the casing required for generator operations?" enquires

Fisher.

"No commander," says von Braun.

"Then team you've got a couple of minutes for the cables only then make double time back to the airlock. Secure your tools out there if needed," Fisher orders.

"Yes sir," Singh acknowledges.

"Is that airlock shutdown yet Lieutenant?" Fisher asks.

"We can't find the problem sir," von Braun responds, "We will need to do a shutdown of the hatch system which will take about an hour."

"That's too late Lieutenant, the CME will arrive within the hour. Close the hatches and shut it down," Fisher orders.

"We will need to put someone in the capsule to close that side of the hatch," von Braun informs.

"Are the assigned personnel there?" Fisher asks.

"Lieutenant's Oliveira and Coulton are assigned to the capsule here, Paton is the other crewmember," says von Braun.

"Paton won't make it, put the other two in the capsule and proceed with the first section of the emergency separation operations. That should be enough to shut down the hatches systems," Fisher orders.

"Yes sir," von Braun acknowledges.

"The team are heading back to the airlock Commander." Jackson informs.

"Fisher to walk team, once you get back in forget re-acclimatisation. Use the portable units to assist us with the last of the Core shut down."

"Aye sir," Singh replies.

"More information coming in from command sir," Jackson interrupts, "The CME is stronger than expected at the front of the incoming wave. In our orbit 600 nT is expected in 60 minutes, 1200 nT in 80 minutes with expected peak intensity of 1700 nT at approximately 120 minutes from now."

"Fisher to von Braun, updated intensity and time. The first major impact will be 600 nT in 60 minutes."

"We are going to have to test on the run commander," von Braun responds. "Has the maximum intensity changed?"

"Still expected at 1700 nT," Fisher informs.

"We will have to calibrate on the run commander," von Braun responds, "It will all have to be done remotely once intensity reaches around 1000 nT as the arms only provide protection to that level outside the elevator capsule."

Unlike on the Enterprise, the exterior of the arms connecting the Ring to the Core of the space stations are more exposed with less exterior shielding. Only the elevator capsule itself has adequate shielding if the doors are closed.

"How soon can you get it up and running?" Fisher asks.

"As soon as the space walk team close the hard hatch on the inside of the airlock."

"As soon as it's closed begin the testing Lieutenant," Fisher orders.

Chapter Five – Solar Emergency

While the Enterprise sits quietly waiting the CME impact to occur, the International Space Station has never more been the hub of activity. With the spacewalk team re-entering the station, the final systems in the airlock are being shut down.

Deputy Chief Engineer von Braun, Lieutenants Doria and Nishizawa and Ensign Yang are in engineering activating the stations Magnetic Shield Generators.

"Lieutenant Volkoff think quick and act fast, you're going to have no more than twenty minutes before closing the elevator door and returning to the Core," says von Braun into the open intercom.

"Aye Lieutenant," responds Volkoff.

"Generators one, three and four are at 20%," Doria informs von Braun.

"Ok. Nishizawa activate the power couplings."

"Power couplings active," Nishizawa informs.

"Yang set unit two computer to synchronise with the other units," orders von Braun.

"Computers synchronising," Yang informs, "Generators Three and Four synchronised, waiting on One."

"Is generator One connected to Three and Four?"

"Yes Lieutenant," says Yang, "They are synchronising through each other but there is no direct path from generator two to one."

"Volkoff, can you do anything about that?" asks von Braun.

"Negative Lieutenant, those cables are on the outside of

the station," Volkoff responds.

"Ok. Brings generator two up to 20% power," von Braun orders.

"Charging capacitor to 20%," Nishizawa informs.

"The capacitor seams stable," says Volkoff.

"Ok, take all of them up to 50% then we will begin to calibrate," von Braun orders.

"Aye Lieutenant," says Doria "capacitor power at 30%, 40%, 50% and stable."

"Volkoff here, the temperature of the power couplings is getting a bit high. I'm going to realign the radiator cables."

"Very Good Lieutenant," says von Braun, "Engineering to Ops, prepare to activate the MSG's at low power."

"We're ready when you are," Fisher responds, "We are currently at 300 nT intensity."

"We are good to about 800 nT then we'll have to bring Volkoff back," von Braun responds.

"We will notify you when we get there," says Fisher.

"Volkoff to Engineering, I've realigned the radiator cables but they aren't having much of an effect."

"Ensign Paton here, the radiator cable needs to be connected to the outer cover of the generator and we didn't get enough time to attach it."

"How are the temperatures Volkoff?" von Braun enquires.

"They are stable at 82 degrees Celsius, but the maximum rating is 85 degrees," Volkoff informs, "The problem is that we will exceed that long before the capacitor reaches 100% charge."

"Can the radiator cable be connected to anything else?" asks von Braun.

"You may be able to connect the cable to the exposed

casing if you can uncover the cable," says Paton, "You can then try jamming the exposed cable to any component that is not the coil or electrical."

"I'll see what I can do over here," Volkoff replies.

"Ops to Engineering, Intensity currently at 600 nT."

"You haven't got long Volkoff, work fast," von Braun orders.

"We are ready for calibration Lieutenant," Yang informs.

"Let's do it. Activate the generators," von Braun orders.

"Generators active," Nishizawa informs.

"Engineering, we are detecting the generators at 400nT on all generators except the outermost detector for generator two, which is at 350 nT on the outside, 420 nT to the forward and 430 to aft," Fisher informs from Ops.

"Yang, rotate the generator negative 50 degrees on the Z-axis," von Braun orders.

"Rotation complete," says Yang.

"Aft and forward corrected to 400 nT," says Fisher.

"Now rotate Y axis negative 70 degrees."

"Outside is now reducing," Fisher informs.

"Correct, Y axis 40 degrees from original," von Braun orders.

"Correcting rotation," says Yang.

"Now it's heading in the right direction," says Fisher.

"Rotation completed," informs Yang.

"Detectors at 390 nT outside, 395 nT inside," Fisher informs engineering.

"That's close enough," says von Braun.

"Lieutenant, the intensity is approaching 800 nT," says Fisher.

"Thanks Ops," says von Braun, "Volkoff time to finish up.

How is that radiator cable looking?"

"I've jammed it in between the upper attachment and the chassis," responds Volkoff.

"Okay, close the door and return to the core ASAP," orders von Braun, "Engineering to Ops, inform the Enterprise we finished calibration and they can activate their generator."

"Will do Lieutenant," Fisher responds in Ops, "Contact the Enterprise Jackson."

"Channel open," responds Jackson.

"Enterprise, Station here," Fisher hails.

"We've got you Station," Foley responds, though the radio channel begins to break up with the slightest amount of static.

"We have completed our calibration and you can activate your generators now," informs Fisher, "We should begin reorientation now."

"I agree," replies Foley, "Did you catch that last message from Houston?"

"Yeah, looks like we will need to lower our orbit faster then we thought. The magnetosphere is collapsing faster than predicted," says Fisher, "We should set a maximum altitude of 300 km and a minimum of 250 km. The shuttles can maintain that range for about two days if needed."

"Sounds about right," says Foley, "If needed we can send the Excalibur over and activate the Enterprise engines if necessary. They have been pre-fired so it shouldn't be a problem."

"Agreed. We should synchronise the shield power up to minimise any potential conflict between the station and ship," says Fisher.

"I'll get Kōno to contact von Braun and make the arrangements," Fisher agrees, "Let's get this re-orientation under way."

Like most spacecraft, both the ISS and Enterprise can use simple Reaction Control System Thrusters to change the direction of each craft. Also known as RCS, each is a simple vent which gas is released from. Each vent points in a particular direction capable of controlling which direction the craft rotates in, and is also capable of providing a limited amount of thrust in situation such as docking manoeuvres. Without the resistance of Earth's dense lower atmosphere, it only takes about one third of a cubic metre of gas to move the massive and heavy station and ship. The rotation occurs at about one half of a degree a minute. The slow speed is for the same reason as the manual docking of Excalibur to Enterprise just the previous day except there is no laser guidance, only a less accurate radar system. Once the manoeuvre is completed, the RCS directly opposite those used in the initial burst vent out the same amount of gas to arrest the rotation. At such a slow rotation, the craft will rotate the required 90 degrees in around 180 minutes.

In the ISS Engineering module, all personnel are still at their stations with Lieutenant Commander Ryan and Lieutenant Volkoff joining them.

"I want everyone to be aware and on guard," von Braun orders, "We haven't had a chance to fully test generator 2. If there are any problems we will have to think quickly and act fast. Lieutenant Volkoff I want you to conduct any remote calibration on generator two that may be needed at the higher power levels."

"Ops to von Braun, I have Lieutenant Kōno for you," says Jackson over the intercom.

"Patch her through," asks von Braun and after a short tone is heard she continues, "Kōno, are you ready to power up the Enterprises shields?"

"Certainly Lieutenant," replies Kōno.

"Okay. We are already on standby at 20%. When we charge our capacitors to full we should increase to 50% over one minute," von Braun informs Kōno.

"That sounds good station. We will wait for your signal," responds Kōno.

"Nishizawa, increase the power flow to the capacitors and charge to full capacity," orders von Braun.

"Parry here, we should aim to cancel out any effects the CME is having on the station. I'll be heading to the comm's module and will monitor the reading from there," says Parry over the intercom, "At the moment I think the generators should be set to 60% to ensure complete coverage of the station within the shield."

"Isn't 50% enough?" asks von Braun.

"Normally they would, but the CME will cause what you could call a cushioning effect. Think of it as placing extra pressure on the shield 'bubble'. That will compress the shield on one side while extending it on the opposite side. The solar arrays are moving into an outward facing position."

"Capacitors at full charge and stable Lieutenant," Nishizawa informs.

"Copy that Parry," says von Braun, "Enterprise, we are ready to begin power up of the shields but our Chief Science Officer suggests we power up to 60% to ensure full station coverage."

"That's okay Station," Kōno responds and after a short pause, "We're ready to begin."

"Begin power up on my mark," von Braun orders, "3, 2, 1, mark."

Initially nothing appears to happen, but after a few seconds a feint harmonic vibration can be heard before the frequency dampeners kick in. Frequency dampeners are normally used anytime there is a vibration on the station. Working in a similar way to Earthquake dampeners used to prevent building damage, these are sphere weights suspended in a fluid which changes into a gas as the forces are dampened. When the gas comes in contact with the edge of the sphere it changes back into a liquid. A sphere is used as a spacecraft can be damaged with vibrations occurring from any direction, while buildings are only damaged from the horizontal motions of Earthquakes. As the magnetic shield generators cause a continual pulsing change in the magnetic field surrounding either of the craft, those pulses begin to cause vibrations on the metal panelling of the craft.

"How is the temperature on generator 2?" enquires von Braun.

"Rising ever slightly, though it doesn't look like anything to worry about," informs Volkoff.

"How are you going Enterprise?" asks von Braun.

"Our generators and systems are stable and we are showing a smooth increase, currently at 48%," replies Kōno.

"We are at 50% now, 15 seconds till targeted power," says Nishizawa.

"I'm seeing the offset that I expected here," says Parry from the comm's module, "60% should do just fine."

"Very good Commander," says von Braun.

"We are now at 60% and holding," informs Nishizawa.

"The temperature on generator two is starting to return to previous levels," says Volkoff.

"Enterprise, we are at 60%," says von Braun.

"So are we Station," Kōno replies.

"I suggest monitoring the intensity of the CME and varying the power level of the shields manually," says Parry, "While the computers should to a good job, if there is a variation of more than 100 nT we could begin to see some harmonics occurring on the outer sections."

"Okay Parry, do you want to head up here to command the team?" offers von Braun.

"That sounds like a plan Lieutenant, I'll be there in a few seconds," responds Parry.

The comm's module and the Engineering module are only one away from each other in the core section with the upper engineering module connected to the external truss. Parry floats through the hatch not long after.

"Volkoff is monitoring generator two, Lieutenant Nishizawa is controlling the power levels. I've sent Yang up to monitor the power systems from upper engineering, Commander Ryan is monitoring the shield geometry and we've got an open channel to Kōno on the Enterprise to synchronise overall power levels," von Braun informs the arriving Parry.

"Very good," says Parry as he gets settled into a spare computer terminal next to Ryan, "I'll monitor the CME intensity from here. If you begin to notice a change in shield geometry without any corresponding change to the power levels, that area is experiencing a higher intensity. You'll need to increase power to the corresponding generators to counteract the effect."

"Sure thing Parry," Ryan says.

"Generator 2's temperature has stabilised Lieutenant," says Volkoff, "It looks like the temperature increases when we increase power to the coils and settles when we stabilise."

"I agree, we should limit increases to 5% a minute in case it gets out of hand," says von Braun, "Engineering to Ops, we are setup here for now. Ryan will take over operations of the shields for as the intensity of the CME increases. I'll stay here to ensure we don't overload the power systems."

"Very good Lieutenant, how's generator two holding up?" asks Fisher.

"Looks like our fix to the radiator worked, although we will need to increase the power gradually to we might fry the generator," von Braun responds.

"Well we don't need that do," responds Fisher, "We are about a third of the way through our rotation. Make sure that the lower generator is stable as it will be taking the brunt of the CME for the next half an hour."

"Will do Commander, Engineering out," replies von Braun.

"Enterprise, Lieutenant Commander Parry here."

"We copy you Parry," responds Kōno as the static increases in the communications channel.

"We only need to synchronise our MSG power levels up to around 80%, after that the 800 meters between us shouldn't make much of a difference," informs Parry.

"Confirm we only need to synchronise to 80, eight zero?"

asks Kōno as the static begins to interfere with the radio communications.

"Eight Zero, 80%," responds Parry, "Parry to Ops. The channel with the Enterprise is getting quite noisy. Any chance of clearing it up?"

"We'll work on it Commander," says Fisher, "But the weather out there is starting to get severe. More like a hurricane then a storm. Maybe increasing the shields will help."

"I'll increase the power up to 80%," Parry says, "But that doesn't help the space between the station and ship sir. That's where the interference is occurring."

"Station to Enterprise, increase shields to eight zero 80% over 4 minutes," Parry asks the Enterprise.

"Eight Ze- -ver four minut-," Kōno responds as the static starts to become overbearing.

"Copy Enterprise," Parry responds, "Increase power Lieutenant with an extra 5% to the lower generator."

"Yes sir," Nishizawa responds.

All of a sudden, a green glow appears on a wall opposite a porthole. von Braun moves to investigate.

Outside the Station, an aurora can be seen dancing in the Earth's atmosphere. The sight, like several endless flags flickering in the breeze, would be a marvellous sight to experience however with Florida in the background von Braun knows better.

"That's Florida outside the station, and there are aurora that far south," expresses von Braun with a slight hint of excitement.

"We will be heading behind the planet in about 8 minutes," Parry replies, "That should give the generators time to cold down before coming out over Africa for another round."

"The temperatures in Generator 2 are rising rapidly," informs Doria while silencing an alarm, "Looks like our fix might not be working."

"What are our power levels at?" enquires von Braun, returning to her workstation.

"They are only at 78%," Parry replies.

"Enterp- -ation, we are detect-," the communications channel cuts out.

"Ops, we've lost the channel to Enterprise," von Braun informs.

"We know, the CME is just too intense to hold it open. We are trying to set up a text link over the fibre cables. Standby," says Fisher.

"It sounded like they might have detected something?" Parry says.

"Perhaps they detected an increase in the CME?" says von Braun.

"We know it's coming," says Parry, "let's go up to full power on the shields just in case."

"Let's do it," von Braun agrees, "Doria, hold back on the power for Generator 2 until the rest are at 100%, then we'll nudge it up from there."

"I'm noticing a impression on the shield geometry lower and space side," informs Ryan, "Generator 2 is rotating to the space side of the station."

"Volkoff, increase power to full on the upper and lower generator," orders Parry, "Ryan re-orient those generators 10 degrees to space side, Doria increase the power to generator two as fast as it can handle it."

"Ops to engineering, we have the text channel open with the Enterprise," Fisher informs.

"Our hands are tied down here Commander, you'll have to relay messages for us," says Parry.

"We are getting some harmonics on the Ring section," says Fisher.

"We have a failure in the frequency dampener in the forward arm," von Braun informs after a quick check of the systems display.

"I can see it from here," Yang says from the upper engineering hatch, "It looks like a containment failure, I can see it venting gas."

"Temperatures are rising in generator 2," informs Doria, "approaching maximum design limit of 95 degrees Celsius."

"We're going to have to shut down the generator, it's next to the dampener," says von Braun.

"If we do that we are going to leave the outer part of the forward ring venerable," says Parry.

"If we don't shut it down we'll lose it all together, Doria begin the shut down sequence on generator two," von Braun orders, "Ops, we have to shut down MSG 2. Evacuate anyone from Ring modules 4 through 12 and close the hatches between them."

"Roger that," Fisher responds.

"Guys, there is something out the window," says Yang.

"Not now Lieutenant," von Braun orders.

"But sir whatever it is it's getting larger."

"Lieutenant-"

"Sir," Yang interrupts, "It's coming from aft of the station... behind our orbit."

"We are beginning to get power interruptions Engineering," Fisher responds as von Braun moves to investigate.

"We have a big gap in the shield and the CME is affecting our solar panels, we have lost about 5% generation capacity," Parry replies, "If it goes beyond 15% it will affect our ability to power the remaining shield generators."

von Braun arrives at the window and sees what looks like a sprite or even a secondary aurora, however it isn't quite in orbit around Earth, almost as if it has a different direction to orbital movement.

"Whatever it is we need to look after our systems, back to your station Ensign," orders von Braun returning to Engineering.

On the Enterprise, science officer Ensign Guang Li is monitoring the medical systems when the module rotates to the aft of orbit. Guang Li is the Chinese contribution to the spaceship program. Having just decommissioning its own space station the Chinese authorities believe this to be a great opportunity to gain experience in space based artificial gravity, while others welcomed the greater cooperation from the Chinese space program and reduction of its reliance on military personnel, with Li being the first non-military astronaut. In response to greater separation with Hong Kong, as a resident Xi was ineligible to enter the Chinese military. However his talents were recognised as being superior to many mainland space program participants so he was granted access to the Chinese space program.

"Li to Ops, there is something approaching us from

behind. It's not quite in orbit with us, it seems too far away," Li observes.

"What does it look like Ensign?" Foley enquires.

"I'm not sure sir, it's not solid. Almost like an aurora the atmosphere is presently experiencing, but it's too far away from the planet," replies Li.

"Do you think it might affect us?" asks Foley.

"Possibly, though it's hard to tell from here."

"See if you can get a better look from another module."

"Sir, it looks like the station is in trouble," says Foster, "They are communicating their shields are failing and they need to lower orbit ASAP."

"How much have we rotated Lieutenant?" asks Foley.

"We are about 13 degrees away from our target orientation," says Foster.

"That should be close enough," says Foley, "Send a message to the station, tell them 'we are ready to begin lowering orbit and we will follow their command'."

"Sending the message sir," Foster replies.

"Shipway, prepare to end rotation and fire engines," orders Foley.

"Solar Array three is beginning to overload," says Yang.

von Braun looks at Parry who slightly shakes his head, providing no alternate action.

"Activate the circuit breakers Ensign," von Braun orders, "Ops, we're pulling the circuit breakers on solar array three or we'll send a surge throughout the station."

"How are our options Lieutenant?" Fisher asks.

"The other generators will go offline within minutes Commander," informs von Braun, "after that, the other arrays will overload and we'll fry the station."

The crew stop for a few moments, coming to a realisation they don't want to. Fisher looks at his First Officer Lieutenant Commander Anton Chertok, seeing the same realisation in his face.

"Chertok, transfer control of the engines to the Enterprise through the fibre link, they may be able to salvage the station. von Braun activate the circuit breakers on the solar arrays and divert internal power to the engines and communication systems," orders Fisher, who opens a station wide communications channel and says with a look of regret, "Attention all crew, this is Commander Fisher, abandon station. Repeat abandon station. This is not a drill. All Crew Abandon Station!"

As Fisher gives the evacuation order and the klaxon evacuation alarm is sounded, an eerie glow begins to appear through the windows on the station.

In upper engineering, Yang looks out the windows to see an amazing sight. The light that was in the distance is upon the station. Varying from red to green and a light blue, the colours dance and twirl around each other like a perfect aurora in space.

"Whatever it is, it's here," Yang says as the first capsule ejects from the station below the Ring.

At that moment the solar array overloads, sending a surge of electricity down the connection truss. Moving like lightning between the metal truss structures, it arrives at the Upper Engineering module.

Then the station begins shaking violently, with the

Enterprise a fraction of a second later feeling the same effect as the aurora engulfs the combined complex.

"Report," Foley orders.

"There is something outside the station causing the vibration Captain but I don't know what it is," Lieutenant Lenz responds, "I'm only getting visual readings with the vibration."

"Sir, the shield generators are beginning to overload," informs Foster.

"Shut them down," Foley orders, "Put the forward camera on the view screen."

As the screen activates, it leaves the Ops crew in awe. What they see almost looks like a submarine pushing itself through a psychedelic body of water, or more accurately a body of charged particles dancing like a flock of migrating birds in the wind.

"Kōno here, if these vibrations get any more intense, we're going to shake more than a few cables lose," comes a message over the intercom.

"The vibrations seem to be stabilising, but certainly not loosing intensity," says Foster.

Then in a fraction of a second the light show stops leaving a black screen.

"What happened to it? Did it pass us?" Foley asks.

"The vibrations are continuing Captain," Lenz says, "They don't match the ships harmonic frequency though so it's still coming from outside."

"What do you think it is Lieutenant?" enquires Fisher.

"I'm not sure, there are no reports of any hull breaches so I don't think it is solid. I'm activating the chemical sensors on the SEV to see if they can tell us anything."

"Sir, we're no longer experiencing the effects of the CME," Foster says, "As the light show cleared so did the radiation sensors."

"How's the station?" Foley enquires.

"We are still getting an active comm link through the fibre cables, but no message has come through since the evacuation message. I'm sending a query through now," Foster replies.

"Lieutenant have you got those sensors online?" asks Foley.

"I'm having trouble getting a radio link to the module," Lenz replies as the vibrations begin to reduce in their intensity, "It looks like whatever was out there has passed."

"Are the frequency dampeners operational?"

"Yes sir," says Lenz.

Foley taps his intercom for a ship wide broadcast, "5 minutes at minimum operations, critical repairs only."

ACT TWO

Chapter Six – Where are we?

The inside of the station is dark. Apart from the odd spark there is virtually no light except a faint glow opposite the windows of each module. As the shaking of the interior equipment stops, only the air circulation systems fans can be heard.

von Braun activates her support pack light and begins to shine some light throughout engineering. The sight isn't pretty. Almost every workstation has some damage to it from the electrical surge that made its way through the upper core.

Another light is seen in upper engineering. As Lieutenant Parry floats back into engineering he activates an emergency power switch. Within a few seconds the workstations begin to power up with some sending out more sparks.

"What's happening up there Lieutenant?" von Braun asks.

"Volkoff and Nishizawa are in the port escape pod but… the surge must have got to them," Parry replies with regret.

"What about the starboard escape pod?"

"It's not attached, they must have gotten away."

"It looks like we have fried the primary computer core," von Braun says switching workstations, "I'm only getting a stand-by signal from the secondary core."

"The secondary core is located below the connection module," Parry responds, "The circuit breakers would have triggered and cut it off. I'll head down and check it out."

"Engineering to Ops," von Braun says into the

workstation intercom, "Ops can you hear me?"

"Looks like the comm lines are down as well," Parry says, "We should use the wireless headsets for now."

"Agreed, I'll be on the primary command channel attempting to contact Ops," says von Braun, "Do a quick check on the network lines computer core before reconnecting it. We don't want to cause anymore problems."

"Will do."

"And if you see anyone else send them up here, I've got a feeling we've got one hell of a job getting even the basic systems online," says von Braun while attaching the wireless headset and selecting the command channel, "Ops this is Engineering can you hear me?"

Fisher, Chertok and Jackson are re-entering Ops when they get the call.

"Fisher here, report."

"The primary computer core is offline and we are working on the secondary computer, environmental systems seem to be operating, the comm lines are down at least in the upper core," von Braun responds, "Once we get the secondary computer core back online I'll have a more comprehensive report. How is the Ring holding up?"

"The systems are running on emergency power. So far it looks like we have no hull breaches as the atmospheric pressure is stable," Fisher replies, "If feels like we may have lost some rotation velocity, maybe 10% but it's manageable. The comm lines are also working fine out here."

"Did the power surge make it too the Ring?" von Braun asks.

"Not as far as we know, our systems seem to be stable with no electrical damage."

"Good, then the circuit breakers did their work."

"Any casualties Lieutenant?" Fisher asks von Braun.

"Lieutenant's Volkoff and Nishizawa sir, they made it to an escape pod but the surge got to them."

Fisher pauses for a second, contemplating what has just happened, "What about the rest of the crew Lieutenant?"

"It looks like Lieutenant Doria and Ensign Yang made it out in the other escape pod. I've got my hands busy here in engineering too check the rest of the Core sir," von Braun replies, "Once Parry has got the computer back online I'll send him down to do an inspection."

"Good idea Lieutenant. Once the computer is back online get the generators up and running," Fisher orders.

"Sounds like a plan Commander," replies von Braun, "I'll inform you when we've got more systems up and running."

"Very Good Lieutenant, Ops out."

"Commander, Lieutenants Unknown and Coulton made it to Ring evacuation capsule 6 and ejected," Chertok informs the Commander, "Ensigns Walsh and Al Majid are moving around the ring checking each module."

"Al Majid to Ops."

"Go ahead," says Fisher.

"I hope you don't think I'm stargazing out the windows Commander but I've notice something very strange."

"Don't keep us in suspense Ensign."

"When that thing hit us, Earth was just coming into view behind module R13," Al Majid replies, "I haven't seen Earth outside any of the windows since we got hit."

"I don't quite understand Ensign."

"Sir, the ring rotates every two minutes. It's been at least ten and I haven't seen Earth or the moon outside any window. We even just past the Lounge and I couldn't see anything outside the observation platform for one full rotation, not even the Sun."

"That's not possible Ensign, we're in orbit around Earth," Chertok responds with a hint of aggravation at such a suggestion.

"Not from what I can see out any of the windows," Al Majid replies.

At that moment, several of the main lights activate.

"Engineering to Ops, we've got the secondary computer core online and about half of the generators active," von Braun informs Ops, "Parry has also reported two more casualties sir. Lieutenant Commander Ryan and Lieutenant Diarra."

"What about everyone else down there?" Fisher asks.

"Lieutenants Oliveira and Rawat and Ensigns Dumas and Paton we're fine in the lower section. Lieutenant Crane and Ensign Watts were able to leave on the shuttle sir," informs von Braun, "It looks like the surge didn't make it past the main engineering module. I've got everyone repairing systems down here now."

"I need the camera systems online as soon as possible Lieutenant, one of the Ensigns is giving me some news that is hard to believe," Fisher orders.

"I'll try to get the lower comm systems patched through sir."

"Commander, I've got some of the cameras on the ring active," Jackson informs the commander.

60

"Let's have a look at them," says Fisher as he moves over to the comms console, "Give me cameras at 90 degree intervals."

"Sir, the comm line on the tether is still active with the Enterprise."

"Can you get a message through to them?" asks Chertok.

"It's still on text mode, I'll see of they can patch through an audio line."

"Have they sent any messages through yet?" Fisher asks.

"The line has only just become active commander, it wouldn't have worked without the computer," Jackson informs Fisher, "I am getting some text through now. They are asking us if we are okay and what is our status."

"Tell then we've lost our main computer core and we are running on generators. No casualties but 4 fatalities including Lieutenant Diarra."

"Aye sir."

"I've got the cameras coming online now," says Chertok.

"The station has informed us they have no casualties, but Diarra has died," Foster informs the Captain, "Three other casualties. They have lost the primary computer core."

"Do they need any assistance?" Foley asks.

"I'm not sure, they want us to establish a full comm channel with them."

"Do it Lieutenant," says Foley, "Any luck with communications from Earth."

"I've still got no signal Captain," Lenz responds.

"I've completed a sweep of the Ring sir," Li says as he

enters Ops, "But I've noticed something else, all the windows are dark."

"What do you mean dark? We are orbiting into the night side of Earth," says Foley.

"That's just it sir, there is nothing but stars out the windows. No Earth, no Sun and no Moon."

"Foster, give me an Earth side camera from the Core."

"Bringing up the camera over the shuttle sir," says Foster as she taps a few buttons her workstation and the view screen activates.

On the view screen is the outer half of the Intrepid ZeroG module and the forward section of the shuttle, but behind it is empty space.

"Have you got the right camera Lieutenant?" enquires Foley.

"Yes sir, the rotation put Earth below the shuttle when we stopped."

"Give us another angle."

Foster taps another button and the screen changes to a camera looking out over the rear of the shuttle from the Core.

"Cycle through all the cameras Lieutenant," Foley orders.

As Foster taps her workstation, various cameras appear on the view screen. A shot facing down the Core angled to view the outer half of the Ring, a shot from the Ring looking down on the fuel pods and engines, another image from behind one of the engine bells directly out into space. All the images show nothing but stars beyond the ship.

"Give me the X and Z axis cameras on the screen from the ring," asks Foley.

The view screen changes to a four-camera window, each

camera directly facing outward from the ring 90 degrees from the next. The officers in Ops scan the view screen for any sign of a familiar object.

"There's the station," Lenz points out.

From the outside, the station looks like it has searing marks on the metal skin surrounding each of the upper core modules. Some of the equipment is sparking on the main truss. Most of Solar Array 3 looks like it's been burnt. Instead of a sparkling gold they have turned a creamy brown colour indicating the silicon and gold have melted together.

"Looks like the upper core took a beating," Lenz says.

"Sir, I've got an audio channel over the comm line open," Foster informs.

"Open a channel," says Foley and continues after a beep from the comms console, "Enterprise to Station."

"We hear you Captain," Fisher replies.

"How are thing over there? Do you need any assistance from us?" Foley asks.

"We've taken a hell of a beating Enterprise, the solar arrays overloaded and sent a surge down the core section," says Fisher.

"We can see the station, you've got some sparking on the truss but it doesn't look like there's any fires or leakages that we can see."

"That's pretty consistent with what engineering are telling me. But we have another, much bigger problem."

"If you're talking about Earth we know," Foley says, "We've just completed a visual sweep and we can't see her."

"What do you think happened?" Fisher asks.

"We don't know Commander," Foley responds, "We were scanning whatever it was that engulfed us. It wasn't solid nor did it affect any of our systems from what we can tell. We tried activating our landing module's sensors but we couldn't establish contact during the radio interference."

"Are you detecting any of the escape craft? Two capsule and the shuttle Constitution were able to eject," Fisher asks.

"We haven't seen them and it doesn't look like they are near the station from out camera angles," Foley replies, "We will keep our ears open and listen for them."

"Captain, the landing module systems are coming online," Lenz informs Foley, "The command must have been sent when the radio interference died down."

"What can you tell me Lieutenant?" asks Foley.

"The external environmental sensors are consistent with deep space sir. The accelerometers aren't detecting any nearby gravity sources."

"So no Earth?"

"No moon either sir, though they are detecting a week pull. Possibly a small nearby body."

"Which direction?"

"Forward of us, at 338 by 344 degrees."

"Do we have a camera pointed out that way?" Foley asks Foster.

"I think so Captain," says Foster as she changes the view screen.

What looks like a normal field of stars to begin with, toward the bottom of the screen a star slightly brighter than the rest can be seen.

"Is that the Sun?" Foley asks.

"It doesn't look like it sir, this star has an orange colour to it. Our sun is yellow even at this size," Lenz informs the Captain.

"The stars look right, I can see plenty of constellations," says Foley.

"I'll see if I can get the spectrometer online, it should give us some more information on that star."

"Very Good Lieutenant," says Foley, "Station, if you need any assistance just ask. We escaped relatively unharmed over here."

"I'll pass the offer onto engineering Enterprise, station out," replies Fisher closing the communications channel.

"Lenz, do you think we can assemble a star chart with our cameras?" Foley asks.

"Only the highest resolution cameras sir, and even then we will still miss some as the sensor will be too small to pick them up."

"Do a quick scan around us Lieutenant. Once that's completed keep the sensors active for longer. That will allow more light to be picked up," orders Foley, "Ops to Engineering, do you have anyone we can spare if the station needs them, they are pretty beaten up over there?"

"Once we bring the systems back online that we shut off for the shields then I might be able to spare one or two," Kōno responds, "They should be done in about an hour."

Chapter Seven – Report

"Engineering, I'm looking at the primary core now," says Lieutenant Parry, "It looks like the fuses on the power system blew and the storage modules look unaffected."

"Thanks Parry, we will look at it later," von Braun responds.

"I've completed photographing the starboard side of the truss sir," informs Ensign Paton, "However the arm is starting to run out of power."

"The batteries were only designed to last for about an hour, how long have you got left?"

"It's down to about 20%, but there is no power coupling active on the truss. I'll need to bring it down to the Engineering module to recharge it."

"Ok Ensign, dock it for recharge," orders von Braun, "Let's take a look at the images you've already taken. Parry head back down here."

"On my way Lieutenant."

von Braun moves to a station with a larger screen and brings up some of the images. Much like the original space shuttle from Earth's history, the arms attached to the station handle most of the external movement of parts, with the transfer platforms taking up the rest. Each arm has a high resolution camera and laser scanner on the end to help with diagnosis.

"Did we get anything from the lasers on the arms?" asks Parry as he moves into position beside von Braun.

"We didn't have enough power for it," responds von Braun as she begins looking over the images of the starboard solar arrays.

"It looks like the Solar Arrays seem fine, we will have to test the motors on them when we get out there," von Braun says as she switches to the next images, "The power and coolant lines also look fine, not splits, kinks or leakages from any of them."

"The radiator also looks undamaged," says Parry.

"There's our first spark," von Braun points out on the screen as the image shows a lit up electrical connection box, "It's on Truss segment S1. I hope you're taking notes Parry, you're going out there to make sure everything is stable."

"Great," Parry sarcastically responds.

"You've got a few hours yet. We've still got to image the port side of the truss and that is where I expect the interesting stuff to be," says von Braun, "Let's see if the radiators are working. Engineering to Ops."

"Go ahead."

"Can you get Enterprise to take some thermal imagery of the upper core section? I want to see where the hot spots are and check if the radiators are still operational," requests von Braun.

"Will do," Fisher responds, "They are also reconfiguring their SEV for maintenance mode and sending it over."

"That will be a great help Commander."

"Anything further to report Lieutenant?"

"We've conducted a preliminary inspection of the primary computer core, it looks like we have only blown the fuses. We've completed an inspection on the starboard truss and will conduct the port inspection when the arm has recharged. So far only limited damage but we need to get out there."

"Who can we send out there?"

"I have already assigned Parry for that. Once we begin the port truss inspection I'll have him suit up."

"Enterprise will send over two crew who will use the suits on the SEV to help out," Fisher informs von Braun, "If you need any supplies they can bring them over at the same time."

"Tell them we will need a few power cables no shorter then 60 centimetres in length and a couple of electrical junction boxes."

"I'll send the message over Lieutenant, Ops out."

The SEV, or Space Exploration Vehicle, is a multi purpose vehicle designed to use in space and on a planet. The forward section contains two seats on a hemisphere window split into 8 sections. The middle of the SEV contains a storage area that doubles as a preparation area for external expeditions as well as the primary airlock off to the port side. The rear contains a working platform with two space suits directly attached to the hull. This eliminates the need for an airlock with the suits hanging from the outside. Once the crew are in the suits, a door closes behind them attaching the backpack. This module of the SEV can be placed atop a variety of other modules. These include a wheeled rover module for use on the surface of an object, an expedition module for use in space on objects like satellites or asteroids and a maintenance module what assists in maintaining the spacecraft. While the SEV has been used on the moon several times, they have been left there. However the Enterprise was to test the first configuration with the SEV as an accent module.

This would remove the necessity to have an additional module during transportation, which would require the crew to transfer materials into for the assent from the surface.

"Here are the cables you wanted sir," Lieutenant Harrison informs Kōno.

"Thank you Lieutenant," says Kōno, "You've been trained to operate the SEV haven't you?"

"I'm the backup crew for the landing team sir."

"Then you'll command the SEV when we send it over. I'm also assigning Lieutenant Pirogov to head over with you."

"Wouldn't you be more qualified sir."

"I would go but I'm needed here. Pirogov has had suit training, you'll just have to pilot the SEV yourself," Kōno replies, "Pirogov is already up there, head to the SEV and load the external boxes with the tools you'll need as well as the junction box and cables."

"Yes sir," Harrison replies.

"Kōno to Ops, Harrison is heading to the SEV now. We've attached the maintenance platform and fuelled it up. It should be about half an hour and they will be ready to depart."

"Very good Lieutenant," Foley responds, "They also need some fuses sent over. Apparently they are starting to run out."

"I'll take them to the SEV now Captain. Kōno out."

"Captain, I've completed a preliminary observation on that star," Lenz informs, "It's definitely a brown dwarf. From what we can tell it's an M3V spectral type and we seem to be about 0.5 AU away from it."

"That's pretty close," Foley says, "What else can you tell

70

me?"

"Not much sir. We'll need to do a star chart comparison before I can even speculate where we are or if there are any planets nearby,"

"How are we going with that Foster?" asks Foley.

"I've got about 70% of the surrounding space imaged sir. From what I can see the constellations look normal so if we have travelled we haven't gone very far," responds Foster.

"What is the lowest magnitude we can see on the images your taking?" asks Foley

"10, maybe 11."

"Alright, when you've completed them put them through the computer. It should be able to match the lower intensity stars and we'll see what's out of place," says Foley, "I'll be in my ready room. You have the conn Ross."

At the far end of Ops is a small office where the Captain of the ship can maintain some privacy while working. While not spacious, the office has a lounge on the wall beside the door. In the middle of the room is a curved desk taking maximum advantage of the limited space. Behind the desk is a comfortable chair for the commanding officer. Foley slumps down into the chair rotating it to the back wall looking out the window. The crew has been at it for more then 14 hours now and even he is starting to get a bit tired. Staring out into space, Foley begins to scan the stars for something out of place and unfamiliar. Spotting Orion, he notices an unusual star above the centre of the so-called belt.

That's not right, there shouldn't be a star there.

Foley turns around and reached for his intercom when the door buzzer sounds.

"Come in!" calls out Foley.

The door opens and Commander Ross enters.

"The SEV is ready to depart sir," Ross informs Foley.

"Very good Lieutenant," says Foley then motions for her to come over to the window, "Come take a look at Orion."

"Looks about right," Ross says after moving over to the observation window.

"Look above the belt Commander."

"You're right sir, I haven't seen a star above it before."

"According to observations there shouldn't be one there, at least not something that is visible if we were still this far away that the constellation still looks normal."

"I'll tell Lieutenant Foster about it," Ross says with a look of concern on her face.

"Something on your mind Commander?"

"This just doesn't feel right. I look out the window and everything looks right. I see familiar stars and constellations. But no Earth, even no Sun. We aren't even detecting any radio signals."

"Hopefully that means we are still close to the Solar System. The stars look too similar to be too far away from Earth and the Solar System. But we aren't close enough to receive strong enough signals from Earth."

"Do you think we could pick up anything from Earth?"

"Only if the transmission is strong and directed toward us."

"So where do you think we are? If the stars are the same then we shouldn't be far away,"

"I'm not sure but it wouldn't be too far, maybe 50 light years," says Ross, "Tell Foster to limit her initial triangulation within that area."

"I'll do that sir," Ross responds, "Commander Fisher would also like you to head over to the station when you can. He's sending the transport pod over."

"He didn't say why?"

"No."

"I suppose it won't do any harm. It's not like I need to be here," Foley says, "Is there anything else?"

"No sir."

"Send the SEV over, we can use the cameras on it to help with the survey of the exterior while they are preparing for repairs."

"I'll let the station know Captain," Ross says as she leaves the room and the Captain returns to gazing out the window.

Chapter Eight – Repairs and Realisation

"SEV to Station."

"von Braun here."

"We are ready to begin infrared imagery of the radiator systems," Harrison informs.

"Okay, let's take a look at them," replies von Braun.

About 6 metres away from the centre of the truss the Enterprises SEV is moving into position. Attached to one of the grappling arms is a camera pack. The camera pack contains three visible light cameras and two heat detecting infrared cameras. One of the two types has a wide-angle zoom lens while the other camera is a close up macro camera. The third visible light camera is a precision magnifying lens.

"We are now in position across from the port radiator panel," Harrison informs, "The camera is active and we are switching the transmission channel to it."

The display in Engineering changes to a black and white thermal image of the radiator panel. As there are no air particles in space for heat to transition to, the radiator panel contains a continuous pipe that loops the coolant liquid back and forth across the panel. This provides the greatest surface area for the heat to radiate out. The truss contains most of the mechanical and electrical equipment for the solar arrays and the coolant prevents these from overheating during maximum energy generation. Various other areas of the station also have radiator panels, though much smaller as they dissipate less heat.

"It looks like we have a baseline temperature of 140 kelvin

to work from. That is what the solar arrays are registering," Pirogov says as he moves the infrared camera across to the port radiator panel.

The image on the screen shows an almost black panel with a hint of the piping crossing up and back down the panel just a fraction lighter than the rest of the panel.

"It looks like there is still some circulation to it," von Braun says, "There is a small area undamaged on Solar Array 4."

"You think its still generating energy from that nearby star?" Parry enquires.

"We won't know that until you test each of the panels manually."

"I've loaded up the equipment bag to take out with me. Anything else you want me to do while I'm out there?"

"We'll find that on the run. Head down to the airlock and finish acclimatisation," orders von Braun, "SEV, I need you to follow the coolant line so we can check where the heat is coming from."

"Which direction do you want us to move Lieutenant?" Harrison responds.

"Move to starboard, the only systems further out on the truss are the solar array systems. If we don't pick up anything along the way then we know its coming from there."

"Okay, we are moving to starboard side at 5 centimetres per second. Tell us if you would like us to stop."

Each of the port and starboard truss segments are a mirror moving out from the centre. On each end is the solar arrays protruding up and down. If you where to look at the truss on its own it would look like a very wide capital letter

H. The next segment in contains the transformers converting the energy generated by the solar arrays into the power used on board the station. The next segment contains the radiator panels pointing out into space away from the station. The panels not only radiate heat out into space using simple transference to whatever is nearby, it can also 'spray' the heat out in any surplus gas, though this also requires the use of the RCS in the opposite direction to maintain the stations position in space. This is not normally required except during maximum operation and sun exposure. The next truss segment contains the pumping stations that transfer the coolant throughout the truss as well as through the core section. The central segment connects the side together and acts as a distribution hub. This segment connects directly to the upper engineering segment.

"SEV, your coming up on the pumping stations. Zoom in on the third pump you come to and hold position when you get to it," orders von Braun.

"When we get to the third pump we'll try and find out why its sparking Ensign."

"I've been thinking about that Lieutenant," Ensign Paton responds, "The pumps were designed to operate on power from any of the solar arrays or from the backup generators. Even though the circuit breakers are still active between the Core and the truss, there might be some energy getting by."

"Well let's take a look," von Braun says as the pump comes up on the display, "It certainly looks like it's getting power from somewhere. There is some heat coming from the power coupling."

"It looks like there is a split cable on the coupling," Paton says as the screen momentarily flashes from the split cable.

"I'll add it to the list for the expedition team to complete," von Braun says.

"You might want to put it near the top Lieutenant. Those pumps don't like being turned on and off. And if the coolant isn't circulating properly it could be freezing up and that will definitely damage the pump if it gets ice crystals in it."

"Good thinking Ensign," von Braun commends, "SEV, continue to the central truss. Try and filter out the flashes caused by the electrical arcing if you can, that's where we have the most problems."

"Will do station," Harrison replies, "I'll apply a filter to the lens."

"Parry to engineering, I'm going to suit up now. We will begin decompression in about half an hour and I can egress about 10 minutes later."

"Very good Parry. I'm sending an updated task list to your computer unit. Use the SEV's platform to transfer to each section faster," replies von Braun.

"Ops to Engineering, are the elevators active yet?" Fisher asks.

"Not yet sir, we don't quite have enough power for them yet," says von Braun.

"Okay, I'll just have to climb up the shaft then."

"What's a bit of exercise sir?"

"Watch it Lieutenant, I'll make you do a few accents once this station is operational again."

"I look forward to it sir."

"The transport pod has docked Commander," informs Foster.

"Ops to Captain, the Transport Pod has arrived," Ross says as she taps the intercom.

Moments later Captain Foley enters the bridge.

"How's that search coming Lieutenant?" asks Foley.

"I've compiled all the images together in a star map," Lenz replies, "but with the primary computer core still offline it will take a while for the secondary core to perform the calculations. Nothing to report yet sir."

"Let us know when you find something Lieutenant," says Foley, "Foster, transfer the elevator to Ring side A12. You have the conn. Walk with me Commander."

Foley and Ross depart Ops moving rearward.

After a moments silence Ross asks, "What do you think Commander Fisher wants to see you about Captain?"

"I'm not sure Commander. If it were anything trivial he would discuss it over the comm link," Foley replies, "How are their repairs going?"

"The SEV has completed its external survey and they are ready to begin the initial truss repairs. They have requested a couple of additional parts and they will be loaded onto the transfer pod by the time you get there."

"Sir, do you think the discussions are going to be about our situation?"

"Possibly, probably," Foley says with a hint of a chuckle, "What do you do when you don't know where you are, what to do or how to get home?"

"You could start by taking an inventory," Ross replies,

"But that would be pretty redundant for us. We haven't actually consumed anything and most of our parts have only arrived in the past few weeks."

"But we do need to know what the station has. I'll arrange a report to be sent over then we can at least start from there."

"I think this ship is going to feel a bit empty," says Ross as she passes empty crew quarters with their doors still open and unclaimed.

"How so Commander?"

"This ship was designed to hold well over 100 people sir. We were even supposed to pick up an extra 10 crew as we passed the Lunar Observatory. That with the last shuttle would have taken us to 40."

"Well depending on the condition of the station me might actually be playing host to a dozen more."

"You don't think we will need to abandon the station do you sir?"

"Who knows Commander? We will have to get us moving eventually and those tethers were only designed to keep us close in orbit. They were never designed to be a tug and even so we would only be able to fire our engines for a few seconds before the station would swing behind us and come into the path of the engine exhaust."

"Could we attach the station to one of the ZeroG module's docking ports? The two sides are identical."

"Possibly, we would then have to take into account a shift in the centre of mass. Get Kōno to do some calculations. The engines can only move about 20 degrees in their configuration."

"Will do," Ross says as they enter the Elevator Transfer

Module.

"I thought it would be spending a bit more time in gravity, oh well," says Foley as he presses the button to open the door, "Head back to Ops Commander. Contact me the moment you know anything about where we are."

"Will do sir," replies Ross as she assists the Captain to strap into the elevators chair.

Each of the Stations massive solar panels are more than 100 metres long and have a surface area of more than 600 square metres. Each panel is capable of generating more than 60 kilowatts (kW) of energy every hour it is exposed to the sun in Low Earth Orbit.

Lieutenant Commander Parry is opening a panel on the initial electrical distribution box just below the motors of Solar Array 2, while Lieutenant Harrison has just finished replacing the same panel on Solar Array 1.

"I have removed the last nut on the exterior panel," Harrison says as he places the nut onto the magnetic tray inside his toolbox. While the toolbox doesn't quite look like the typical metal or plastic box with straight sides, it resembles more of a cooler bag. The padding on the outside is designed to prevent any damage to equipment if it bounces off it in the weightlessness and lack of gravity in space. It does however contain many magnetic plates inside designed to hold tools and equipment without fear of losing them, though that does not stop them coming loose some of the time.

"Ok Harrison, stow the driver and you can then remove

the panel," von Braun replies. Even though the station is nowhere near Earth, items still need to be kept track of. Especially when there isn't much hope of getting another spanner delivered if one does become lost.

"I've stowed the drive and am proceeding to remove the panel," Parry says. After a few seconds he continues, "I've removed the panel and giving it to Harrison."

The inside of the box looks like any electrical distribution box, though lacking circuit breakers you might see on Earth.

"The visual inspection looks the same as Array 1. I can't see any burn marks. I'm going to begin inspection with the Current probe," Parry says.

The Current probe is about 20 centimetres long resembling a screwdriver. The handle has a couple of LED lights to indicate whether current is detected and how strong. The probe is used to ensure there is no broken insulation that may cause electrocution.

Harrison hands Parry the probe and begins inspecting the electrical lines.

"Once again just like Array 1. We are picking up some current through the electrical connectors," informs Parry, "The loading checks out. I'll put a meter on it and get a more exact reading."

Parry passes the probe back to Harrison and takes out a multimeter. He attaches it to the side of the box and places two leads on a set of wires.

"I'm getting a reading of 150 Volts at just under 2 kW on the left panel," says Parry as he switches the leads to the next set of cables, "The same on the right."

"Do you think that star might be sending enough energy

out this way to be generating that amount of electricity?" Ensign Paton asks in the ISS engineering, "These are the undamaged arrays."

"Possibly Ensign but we will need to know more about it before coming to any conclusion," von Braun replies, "Ok Parry, you can replace the cover then move on to the interim transformer."

The interim transformer combines the energy from both solar arrays into a single electrical feed.

"I'll take the driver Lieutenant," Parry requests.

"Do you want me to move down to the transformer Commander?" Harrison asks as Parry screws the remaining nuts into their bolts.

"Definitely. It's been three hours already and I want to complete the inspection on the radiator before we have to wrap up today," Parry responds, "Check the flow on the radiator cables as you head down. I want to make sure they aren't blocked."

"Yes sir," says Harrison as he rotates about 90 degrees clockwise and begins floating down to the next section of the truss.

Moving down the truss Harrison to use a vibration sensing strap to check that the liquid coolant is moving through the pipe as the gloves on the space suit reduce the ability to sense the vibrations as one normally would with their bare fingers. While the strap can't quite detect blockages, unusual vibrations are a signal something isn't quite right.

"I've replaced the cover Station and stowed the driver," Parry informs, "I'll now move down to the transformer."

Chapter Nine – Making Plans

As the door on the transport pod opens Captain Foley can smell that the station has been through quite a lot. Any engineering student never forgets the smell of burning metal caused by electricity.

Seven hours and the environmental systems still haven't filtered it out.

"Welcome to the International Space Station Captain, though I think we need to call it something a bit more then 'International' now," Commander Foster says floating into the core module, offering his hand to Foley.

"Permission to come aboard Commander." asks Foley.

"Granted," Fisher says with a firm handshake.

"It's been a while since I was here," Foley says.

"Four years wasn't it Captain?" asks Fisher as he motions upward of the Core.

"And I wish I could say she doesn't look a day older. So how are your systems?"

"Not much has changed since our last update. We are conducting the inspection on the starboard truss right now and it seems as though it's relatively undamaged."

"That's good news Commander."

"That it is. It looks like the panels are still generating some energy from that star so we won't have to completely rely on the generators."

"We have the same on the Enterprise. Obviously we are in better shape but we are generating about 10 kW."

"We are getting about 2 kW out of each array. We haven't looked at the port side yet and that's the damaged side."

"Is 4 kW going to be enough for the station?" Foley asks.

"I've got my deputy chief engineer working on that, but it doesn't look promising," Fisher responds, "In fact that's why I called you over here."

"I was wondering what you wanted to see me in person for."

"At such a low power level we won't be able to keep all our systems powered all the time. I was thinking we might be able to transfer some modules over to the ship. They should attach to all the ZeroG modules without any problems."

"I've got my team working on that too Commander. I was thinking we will eventually need to move both the ship and station and those tethers were never designed to be towing cables. If we attach the station to one of the modules it will give us a more solid structure to move."

"So you want to move us Captain?"

"Once we find out where we are and what our direction and velocity in relation to the star we can move closer. We are only about 0.5 AU away from it and the closer we are the more energy the Solar Arrays will generate."

"I suppose you're right Captain. It's just with all the repairs were doing over here my mind is a bit pre-occupied."

"We're all feeling a little bit guilty over there. We haven't got much to do while you guys are running about and repairing the station."

"At least you can be our eyes and ears for us," Fisher asks, "Any sign of the escape pods?"

"We've been listening for any signals but so far we aren't picking anything up."

"I hope that's a good thing. At least they might have gotten away before whatever brought us here hit us. Any idea on what it was?"

"None yet. It wasn't solid and the gas sensors didn't pick up anything though they were set for atmospheric detection in Earth orbit. I suppose we can just call it an 'Anomaly' until we've got a better name for it," Foley says.

"May as well, we've got no idea over here," Fisher responds as they enter Engineering, "Captain Foley may I introduce you to my deputy chief engineer Lieutenant Anna von Braun."

"Lieutenant," Foley says as he shakes von Braun's hand, "I think you're not only living up to your great grandfathers reputation but if you can get this station back up an operational you'll exceed it."

"Thank you Captain," says a flattered von Braun as she turns to Fisher, "Commander, we've completed the inspection on the interim transformer and it checks out. It seems to be transferring power to the radiators, which is causing them to circulate."

"Very Good Lieutenant. Will you be conducting any further inspections today?"

"We are going to have a look at the radiator then call it a day. We will then head back out and continue across the truss tomorrow."

"How long will it take?" Fisher asks.

"Only about an hour Commander, after that I'll bring Parry back in. It's been a long day."

"That it has Lieutenant," Fisher responds stretching a bit.

"Have all the preliminary visual inspections been completed?" Foley asks.

"They have and we don't have any major damage. We lost the fluid from one stabilisers on the Ring arm but it's empty and has been shut down," von Braun replies.

"We don't even have a spare one of those on the Enterprise," says Foley.

"I've shut down elevator operations and when we do reactivate that arm we will have to conduct speed tests. Those stabilisers help smooth out any vibrations caused by the elevators movement," says von Braun.

"Ops to Commander," Jackson calls over the comm system.

"Fisher here."

"We have a message from the station for the Captain," informs Jackson.

Captain Foley nods.

"Put it through Lieutenant," Fisher replies.

A beep is heard and Foley acknowledges, "Foley here."

"Captain, we know where we are," Ross says.

A look of intrigue appears on the crew's faces.

"Don't keep us waiting Commander," Foley edges.

"Combining the data we are collecting on the star and the apparent movement of the star charts we believe we are in Gliese 581."

"How sure are you Commander?" Foley asks as the crew begin to look excited.

"The data we have collected on the star, combined with the movement of several stars from one side of the star chart to the other suggest so Captain," Ross replies, "We even think we have detected a few of this star systems planets."

"That puts us at what, 20 light years away from Earth?" Foley enquires.

"That's right sir."

"20 light years, how did we travel 20 light years in just a couple of minutes?" Fisher exclaims.

"Thank you Commander, continue your efforts. We need to know exactly where we are and if we are traveling anywhere. Foley Out."

"Well that was something different," says Foley as he steps down from a ladder, "That was one thing I never did when stationed here."

"If von Braun can't get the elevator operating on the opposite arm you'll have to climb all the way back up," replies Fisher as he dismounts the same ladder shortly after, directing the two to walk around the ring, "Gliese 581. What do we know about it?"

"From what I remember it's a brown dwarf system. Five confirmed planets with three possible others. Of those, 5 of the planets are thought to be in the inner planetary system about 0.25 AU from the star, with the next closest at around 0.75 AU."

"So if our readings are correct we're about right in the middle of them."

"Seams so. We should be clear of any asteroids though, this systems belt starts at around 25 AU out."

"Any planets in a habitable zone?"

"Three of them, I think Gliese 581 g is smack bang in the middle."

"That's promising," Fisher says, "You think it could harbour any life?"

"I don't remember hearing much about the composition

of either the planet or its atmosphere," responds Foley, "Only the few closest planets to the Solar Systems have any meaningful information catalogued."

The two commanders arrive at the stations Ops deck.

"Anything to report Lieutenant?" Fisher asks.

"Engineering reports the inspection has cleared the radiator on the starboard truss. Lieutenant von Braun is ending the walk for today," Jackson replies.

"Thank You Lieutenant," says Fisher, "Join me in my ready room Captain?"

As the two enter the ready room, some of Commander Fisher's mementos have fallen from their benches. A Soyuz and Orion Capsule, Dream Chaser and an S37-D.

"I've flown in each of these craft," says Fisher as he gathers the models, "not once did I think I would end up all the way out here."

"Yeah. All I was hoping for was one of our neighbouring planets," Foley says as he moves over to the windows, "I certainly wasn't expecting a neighbouring star system."

"Neighbouring. You call 20 light years 'Neighbouring'?"

"When you look at the size of the galaxy, even our spiral arm, 20 light years is barely our backyard."

"What's the top speed of that ship of yours?"

"You know speed is relative," Foley responds, "She is designed to get us from Earth to Mars in two months."

"Any idea how long it would take to get home?" Fisher asks.

"You've got me on that one Commander," Foley replies, "That's something you'll have to ask the computers."

"Once Parry is back inside I'm going to order a break," Fisher says, "It's almost been a day since I've had any sleep and I know most of the crew aren't that far behind."

"It's the same on the Enterprise, though we did get a rest after aligning the shields," Foley responds, "What happened over here?"

"We didn't get that shield generator installed fully in time. We had to leave the external panel off and that's the radiator for that component. Then improvising we jammed the radiator cable into the cover over the stabiliser."

"I'll take it didn't handle the heat?"

"No. She burst and vented all the gas out into space. We should do fine with one elevator given we're in the middle of a crew transfer. It's a shame they didn't do a simple person for person swap."

"Well you need the space encase we needed to get off the Enterprise during shakedown."

"I suppose so. Drink?" Fisher offers Foley.

"Not this time commander," Foley replies taking a bottle of water instead, "Besides I've got a feeling that's going to become a precious commodity around these parts. Not unless you've got a secret stash of potatoes hidden somewhere around here."

"You thinking about brewing some moonshine Captain?"

"As I said, 'precious commodity'."

"If not a motivational reward."

"I think we're going to need some of those too."

"Too us," Fisher toasts holding up his drink, "Earth's first motley crew of explorers."

"Too us."

The commanders bring their drinks together taking a swig.

"Talking about potatoes, we don't have any but we do

have that seed bank on the Dutch ZeroG module," Fisher says pouring another drink, "We could hook up a hydroponic system, maybe funnelling our water supply through it before putting it through the recycling system."

"You know there are people on Earth who would think that's disgusting?" Foley says.

"There are people on Earth who don't even believe we recycle every drop of water we release. Whether it's from the air, the laundry system or out toilets."

"I'm drinking that water here," Foley abruptly stops taking a mouthful from his bottle, "We should do it though, putting it through the plants will extend the life of the filters."

"Do you think we can do it? I mean attach the station to the Enterprise and still move it," asks Fisher.

"Maybe, but we might have to salvage parts of the station too and retrofit them to the station," replies Foley.

"You're not thinking about leaving the station out here on her own?" enquires Fisher with a look of concern.

"If it is what must be done," says Foley.

"If I was in charge I wouldn't leave her," states Fisher with a bit of arrogance, "I've been her commander since you left four years ago. Besides, there's plenty of space and systems she has to offer."

"We'll cross that bridge when we come to it commander, let's first get this station back up and running before we make any rash commitments," says Foley trying to reassure the Commander, "It is your station after all."

Chapter Ten – Diagnosis Terrible

"Captain on Deck," says Lieutenant Foster as Captain Foley enters Ops on the Enterprise.

"I hope everyone had a decent rest last night," says Foley, "we've got a lot of work to do today. Commander, my ready room."

The Captain and Lieutenant Commander Ross enter the ready room.

"There's quite a bit to do today Commander," Foley says as he takes his seat, offering the couch opposite to Commander Ross, "The Station will be completing it's inspections today and I want the SEV back over there."

"Harrison and Pirogov are ready to head back over sir," says Ross, "They are loading a few more parts to take over and they will depart when that's finished."

"Very good. Now we've got all our repairs complete I want to focus our efforts of this star system. I want to know everything we can find out. What our position and velocity is, how many planets this system really does have, what their surface is like and begin working on a plan to take us through the system."

"Through the system sir?"

"Yes Commander. Home is only about 2 degrees above the system. We've only got three options and I don't think floating out here doing nothing for the rest of our lives is the option we're going to take."

"Yes sir."

"I also want to get engineering working on the best way to attach the ship and station. Commander Fisher and I we're working on an idea to help provide some palatable food. They have the seed bank over there and each species has at least 1000 seeds. If we can setup a hydroponics cultivation system we can pre-filter our existing water supplies before recycling."

"Ingenious solution sir. We should be able to salvage a dozen metres or so of spare piping from somewhere of either craft."

"Captain, Commander Fisher is contacting you sir," informs Foster.

"Is there anything else Commander?" Foley asks Ross.

"I've got our inventory list ready sir," Ross says handing the Captain a data drive, similar to an old USB flash drive from the 2010's.

"Thank you commander, you're dismissed," says Foley moving his attention to his computer, "Good morning Station, did you get a good nights rest?"

"Surprising good Enterprise. Not much seemed to go bang during the night, though trying to sleep in 0.85 gravity is a bit of an experience," replies Fisher.

"I can imagine. The SEV is being loaded with supplies and will depart within the hour."

"Thank you Captain," says Fisher, "Do you mind if I head over today Captain?"

"Something else on your mind Commander," enquires Foley.

"You could say that Captain."

"Then I look forward to seeing you sometime today Commander," says Foley, "We'll be continuing our survey of the star system and hopefully we'll have a better picture of the local situation by the end of the day."

"I look forward to hearing all about it Captain," says Fisher.

"Oh and it's B.Y.O. over here Commander."

"I get the hint Foley. Station Out," says Fisher leaning back in his chair.

I've only got two bottles left. Four years into a five-year mission and out of three cases of rum only two bottles left.

The door to the Commander's ready room chimes, "Enter."

The stations first officer, Russian Lieutenant Commander Anton Chertok enters. Even though the preceding 30 years has seen numerous nations and even private companies enter space flight, the United States and Russia still dominate the missions with their established commands. Unlike the normal tik-tok cycle, Chertok had been assigned by the Russian Federal Space Agency as their second first officer in a row. As part of a rotation agreement the position of Commanding Officer was given to another participating nation, this time the British. Even though Chertok was hoping to obtain the C.O. position, he didn't let the disappointment show in his duties or interactions with the crew.

"Commander, Parry is suiting up in the airlock again for today's walk. He is hoping to get a head start as soon as he can get out there."

"As long as he doesn't need the SEV and it's crew then that shouldn't be a problem."

"No sir. They should both arrive at the same time," says Chertok, "I took a walk around the ring last night and inspected the rotation engines. They look like they are operational and we should have enough fuel on the ring side to speed up our rotation."

"Very good. We'll wait until the initial repairs are completed to the core before attempting a greater rotation."

"I worked with the core night watchman to get another optical communications cable operating over to the Enterprise so we can increase our capacity as soon as they are configured over there."

"Anything else Commander?"

"No sir."

Fisher rotates his chair to the window.

"Is there anything else sir?" Chertok enquires.

"I've been thinking about the command protocol here," says Fisher, "We're in the middle of nowhere, no communications with Earth and it looks like we are going to combine our craft and crew at some point soon."

"Wouldn't the protocol be the highest rank has command?"

"Yes. But even though Foley technically outranks me, his rank is based on his position as commanding officer of a ship. His commission rank is still Commander and there's our dilemma."

"Who is the most senior sir?"

"By commission date it looks like I'm senior," Fisher says.

"But that's not what concerns you?"

"No. I don't know anything about that ship, and I'm sure there's some regulation somewhere that states you can't just depose a ships commanding officer because you have seniority."

"But these are exceptions circumstances commander. If we are going to combine at some point we need a united crew."

"Yeah, that's why I'm heading over there later today," says Fisher, "We need to have the discussion at some point. We may as well start it now."

"How do you think he will take it sir?" Chertok asks.

"We won't be a crew until we're all in one vessel," Fisher replies, "Plenty of time to talk it over and make a decision."

An alert shows on the ISS airlock panel indicating depressurisation complete, which von Braun dismisses and opens the inside hatch.

As she moves inside to help Lieutenant Commander Parry with the removal of his suit they begin discussing the damage on the port truss.

"Even if you could get the radiator active, both the solar arrays are basically fried," says Parry, "The silicon has crystallised. Even if they were closer to the star they are too fragmented to cause any charge fragmentation. We weren't even reading any voltage or current on the contact grids."

"Great, so that means we've only got half the truss," von Braun responds a little agitated.

"One active truss," replies Parry, "Once we can power on the components on the port truss we will know how many parts we have. We may even be able to move one of the arrays from the starboard side for more efficient power generation."

"That's only if that power surge didn't knock anything out

that can't be swapped. We only have one radiator on each side and if it's gone," says von Braun.

"How is the assessment going Lieutenant?" Commander Fisher asks as he floats into the airlock module.

"Basically we've only got half the truss sir," von Braun responds, "We've checked out all the equipment. The port solar arrays are damaged beyond repair and are useless. Once we complete the final inspection on the upper engineering module, we'll be able to reconnect the circuit breakers to the starboard truss then begin putting power into the port truss systems to find out what's working."

"When can we boost the Ring rotation back up to 2.5 revolutions?" enquires Fisher.

"We will need at least 5 kW of power to achieve that," says von Braun, "The port panels are only generating about 4 kW and we won't be able to take power from any other systems."

"What if we connect the station to the Enterprise? Would they be able to transfer the extra power?" suggests Fisher.

"Maybe if we left one of the tethers attached. But they were only designed to transfer power from the station to the ship while it was under construction," says Parry, "Depending on where we attach we might need to connect two of them together to reach each other."

"I'm heading over to the Enterprise now. I'll see what they have to say over there," says Fisher as he pushes off floating down to the ZeroG modules.

"That's going to be one awkward conversation," says von Braun.

"What, connecting the station and ship?" replies Parry.

"Oh, you have been out there all day," says von Braun

stowing parts of the space suit away, "Rumour has it the Commander and First Officer had a conversation about command this morning."

"Chertok isn't going to commit mutiny is he?" enquires Parry.

"Not our command. If we do combine then we're going to become one crew and we can only have one CO," says von Braun, "That's going to be one interesting conversation."

Like all docking operations, the final few meters of the Transport Pods docking is almost as slow as any unattached craft. The Transport Pod is able to use the cables to guide it into place and assist with manoeuvring. Once the pod docks to the station, it takes only a minute to pressurise the airlock between then.

As Commander Fisher opens the pods door Lieutenant Kōno is waiting for him on the other side with the ships door already stowed.

"Permission to come aboard Lieutenant?" Commander Fisher requests.

"Permission granted Commander, welcome back," Kōno replies.

"I was expecting to meet the Captain."

"Captain Foley requested that I meet you here sir," responds Kōno, "I'll escort you to the elevators."

"Lead the way," says Fisher.

"von Braun contacted me while you were on the way over," says Kōno floating up the Core, "She says you want to connect the ship and station together."

"That's something I'll discuss with the captain today Lieutenant," replies Fisher, "But we do need extra power to increase the velocity of our Ring back up to 2.5 RPM. Have you been thinking about how it could be done?"

"It's going to be tricky Commander. The only place we can actually fit the two together is connecting the ventral docking port of the station to the outside of one of our ZeroG stacks. But we'll have a huge centre of mass problem and our engines won't be able to compensate for it."

"That will be a bit of a problem. Is there anyway the station could be attached to the front of the shield? There is a docking port up there isn't there?"

"There is sir but if we're going to move we won't be able to cover that part of the shield until the station is moved and even then the station itself would be venerable being in front of the shield."

"There is no way we could wedge the station somewhere in between the core modules?"

"Only in the most desperate of circumstances Commander," Kōno chuckles, "Some of the systems and connectors are incompatible and I don't think we would even have enough spare patch cables to do it, even if the station was in perfect condition."

Kōno and Fisher float through the porthole into the connection module.

"Kōno to Ops, Commander Fisher is ready to head down the Elevator," Kōno says into a comm panel.

"Thank you Lieutenant. I'll meet the Commander in R11," Foley responds.

"Here you go sir," Kōno directs Fisher to the appropriate elevator.

"Will you keep looking into how we can combine Lieutenant? The last thing I want is to leave the station out here," Fisher asks as he straps into the elevator seat.

"That's what the Captain has me working on Commander," Kōno replies, "The moment I come up with any more ideas I'll let you know."

"Thank you Lieutenant," Foley says as he pushes a button on his chair arm and the door closes.

Chapter Eleven – Commanders Meeting

"You want to talk about this now?" Foley says with a more than slightly raised voice, "You haven't even begun repairing the station yet and you want to talk about who is in command."

"Given that we are talking about combining the station and ship we need to start having this discussion," Fisher responds.

"And what exactly prompted you think we need to have this discussion," Foley enquires, "We are cooperating with each other on repairs, spare parts, supplies."

"Even so, Commander Chertok and I-"

"Chertok," Foley interrupts, "Your taking advice from the person who tried to cut your command short so he could take command of the station."

"No," Fisher sternly replies, "I bought the issue up with him this morning during our daily briefing."

Foley turns around and stares out through his ready room window into space, his body language indicating he is yet to calm down.

"Listen Captain, I know it is tough to talk about. You've only just taken command of the Enterprise," says Fisher, "And you're doing a fine job. But the way things are going, especially with the power situation over there we need to have this discussion sooner than later."

"You need people who know this ship Commander," says Foley, "We've had more than 4000 hours in the simulator preparing for every situation and scenario."

"And what have those simulations told you about our

situation?" Fisher asks.

"Repair the ship and set course for home," Foley replies, "But they never thought something like this would happen."

"We're nowhere near the time we need to combine our crew Captain," Fisher says, "When that time does come I'm going to need all the help I can get. While the station and this ship are similar in design, neither my crew nor I know much about operating this ship. We may have helped assemble her and turned the switch on, but operations is what your crew are for."

"Until then?" Foley asks.

"Until then we are our own crews, and until we come up with a viable plan to attach the station and ship that's not going to happen," Fisher reassures.

"If there isn't anything else Commander, I'll authorise the transfer of parts over to the station," says Foley.

"That's all for now Captain," Fisher says.

"Kōno might be able to arrange for you to take some parts with you," says Foley as he turns his attention to his computer and Commander Fisher turns and leaves the ready room.

"Ross to my ready room," Foley says into his comm panel. A few second later the ready room door opens and Commander Ross enters.

"The hide of that man," Foley says with a cross of anger and disappointment.

"Commander Fisher said you might have a temper when he walked past," Ross replies.

"You know what he just wanted to discuss?" Foley asks rhetorically, "He wanted to talk about command."

"It was something I was thinking about Captain," Ross replies.

"Not you too."

"Well Captain, if I may?"

Foley nods.

"We are all alone out here. We have no mission control and very few personnel. It was only a matter of time before it came up."

"Yeah," Foley exhales, "I was just hoping it would take a bit longer. It's not like we aren't cooperating."

"That's what we've been trained to do sir. Help out others if there are any problems or emergencies. We learnt that for the original International Space Station," Ross says, "What did he have to say about it?"

"Oh, that once we become a combined crew we will need to sort it out," responds Foley, "But I know the protocol. Seniority and service time."

"Who has those sir?" asks Ross.

"Who do you think?" says a dejected Foley.

"We aren't supposed to do multiple trips down the arms so close," says Captain Foley.

"Don't worry about it sir," Kōno replies, "We can handle it twice a day if necessary."

"I learnt from my time on the station that twice a week is enough to upset me," says Foley.

"Well they are still having troubles with their communication systems over there and they can only receive one video feed at a time," says Kōno.

"At least we know it's not our side," says Foley, "At least he agreed to have morning briefings every day. Are you sure this is the only option we have Lieutenant?"

"von Braun and I were up late last night and it's the best option," Kōno replies, "The forward docking port isn't compatible with any of the ports on the station and I'm not about to pull this ship apart and squeeze the station. We haven't even had the chance to put the ship through it's paces on it's own."

"Ops to Engineering, the station is ready," Foster informs.

"Patch them down here Lieutenant," Foley replies.

After a couple of seconds the monitor changes to a view of the Enterprise engineering with Commander Fisher and Lieutenant von Braun.

"I've called this conference to discuss our options for moving forward," Foley starts, "Commander Fisher and I discussed yesterday that we will need to combine the ship and station into a single craft before we begin moving either. Our Chief Engineers have been discussing the issue and they have come up with a solution. Lieutenant."

"Lieutenant von Braun and I discussed the most practical solution. Given we are actually drifting away from the Gliese 581 star, we need to at least arrest the drift, if not move closer to generate more power," Kōno says, "As a result, we have come to the conclusion that we should connect the station to the Enterprise through the ZeroG platforms on both craft."

"I thought we were going to have a centre of mass problem Lieutenant?" Fisher asks.

"That was assuming we connected the station to the ship using the ventral docking port," replies Kōno, "however we believe we can connect a ZeroG module from either craft to each other, bringing the centre of mass much closer than where it was going to be."

"Is that going to be enough to compensate for any drift?" enquires Foley.

"It will compensate for most but we will only be able to use the engines in short bursts of about 5 minutes each," says Kōno, "After each burst we'll use the RMS to manoeuvre the combined craft back in the appropriate direction. We'll have to start about 5 degrees off the direction we want to travel in and as the craft rotates we will eventually have the correct velocity in the right direction."

"How long will it take to arrest the orbital drift?" asks Fisher.

"We will need to conduct about 12 bursts to get us into a stable orbit around Gliese 581," says von Braun, "After that we can decide on a more permanent solution of the craft."

"Will the ZeroG stacks be able to handle the shift in mass as we change our velocity?" Foley asks.

"Not on their own, however Lieutenant von Braun has come up with a temporary but unusual solution," says Kōno.

"We will use the tether cables connecting the two craft to cradle the station," says von Braun, "Once our velocity changes it will allow us to distribute the force to another section of the station and ship."

"Do you know exactly how you'll do that?" enquires Fisher.

"We're still discussing whether to loop the tether through

an open section on the parabola shield frame or some other part of the ship, though that seems the most likely," replies von Braun.

"Will the parabola frame be able to handle the force?' asks Foley.

"It should be able to sir, given that the centre of mass will be quite close to the ship. We should be able to use some of the craft attached to the station if it needs a bit of a boost," replies Kōno.

"That might work, but it would be more comforting if we had the shuttle over here on the station. That would provide a greater boost when needed," says von Braun.

"Ok, we'll begin working on it Station," says Foley, "How are your repairs coming along?"

"We've got about 70% of the circuit breakers reconnected to the starboard truss. Once they are all active we'll test our the equipment on the port truss to see what's operational," Fisher responds, "But if these repairs don't go smoothly we'll need to connect together soon. We're beginning to lose rotation on the Ring over here. If it slows down below 1.75 RPM she'll begin to seize up."

"Good luck station. Don't forget we are here if you need any help," says Foley.

"Appreciated Enterprise, Station Out," says Fisher as the screen goes blank.

"That was a lot less painful than I expected," says Foley.

"In what way sir?" asks Kōno.

"After our little discussion yesterday I thought things might start changing," responds Foley, "Get to work on the attachment procedures Lieutenant."

"Aye sir."

"That's the last of the circuit breakers," says Parry from outside the upper engineering module, "How are the systems looking?"

"The distribution grid is operating as it should. We are getting about 3.9 kilowatts into the station," von Braun replies, "With the radiator active that makes 4 kilowatts."

"Sounds good," Parry responds.

"If you want to start checking the circuit breakers on the port side we can see if we'll need to patch across from outside the station or not," von Braun orders.

"Okay, heading that way now," says Parry.

"Engineering to Ops, we've got the starboard truss up and running," says von Braun into her intercom.

"Very good Lieutenant," Chertok responds, "What's next?"

"We are going to check the circuit breakers on the port side," von Braun responds, "If they are undamaged we'll be able to reroute the power from inside the station to test the equipment on the port truss."

"Sounds like a plan. How is Commander Parry going out there?" asks Chertok.

"It's his third straight day on a spacewalk but he is holding up well," von Braun responds, "We will only need the SEV when we test the port truss so he will have at least a day off."

"Good. How's the progress on craft attachment going?"

"I'm getting updates every couple of hours from the Enterprise. We should be able to complete the integration with two days."

"Good to hear, I'll inform the Commander. Ops out."

"I'm on the port side now Lieutenant," Parry says over the intercom, "It looks like the circuit breakers did activate but the current must have been too strong."

"So that's why we got a surge down the station," says von Braun.

"It looks like it. I'll begin testing them and if they can handle the load I'll mark each breaker for reset."

"Ops to von Braun, I've got a communication for you from the Enterprise," Jackson says over the intercom.

"Patch it through," responds von Braun as the video activates, "What can I do for you Lieutenant?"

"I've gone over all possible combination of connections. I think it's best if we connect the two European ZeroG stacks together," informs Kōno, "They have the most spare power connections and we'll be able to transfer about 2 kilowatts through them."

"Sounds good. They have a direct connection to the lower Core's energy transfer grid left over from construction of the station," says von Braun.

"Do you think you will be able to retract the damaged solar arrays?" asks Kōno.

"I'm not sure we can get power to the retraction motors yet. I've got someone out there now checking the circuit breakers to that side," replies von Braun, "If we can't we'll have to manually wind them back. That will take a full day to do each array."

"It will give us a bit more movement during acceleration. Solar Array 2 is the one that will need retracted," says Kōno.

"We'll focus on that array first Lieutenant," informs von Braun, "Any word yet on where you want each of the capsules and the shuttle?"

"We are working on that now. I'll get back to you in the morning when we have a solid plan. Enterprise Out."

Chapter Twelve – Realisation

"So this is the plan I can send over to the station?" Captain Foley asks during the morning ships meeting in his ready room.

"Yes sir. That's the configuration we'll need to achieve to have the least structural impact during acceleration," replies Kōno through the computer display on the wall.

"Okay, I'll transmit it over to the station. Thanks Lieutenant."

"So we're really going to do this?" asks Ross.

"Hey, if it we're up to me I would cut the station loose and head for home," says Foley, "But he could pull rank at any moment then the decision would be out of my hands."

"I still can't believe this is what Commander Fisher wants," says Ross.

"That man can be stubborn. Watch out for that when he finally does head over here," says Foley.

"Captain, I have Commander Fisher calling from the station," Foster informs over the intercom.

"Start getting the ship ready. I've got a feeling he wants to move quickly. That will be all Commander," says Foley as he turns his attention to the computer on his desk.

"Captain, how is the morning over there?" Fisher asks.

"Sometimes I think we need to call it something different when we are in space," says Foley, "Morning, Afternoon, Evening, Night."

"Without the sun moving it does sometimes feel a bit redundant," agrees Fisher.

"I've got the final procedures drawn up to attach the ship

and station together," says Foley as he pushes a few buttons and transmits the information over to the station.

"We might need to do it very soon Captain. We've lost even more rotation over the past day and we're down to about 2 RPM. It's starting to get a bit light headed over here."

"As long as you guys agree to the procedures we can begin some preliminary tasks, even manoeuvring the two craft closer together."

"We'll take a look and if we can we'll be in contact as soon as possible," says Fisher, "I was chatting with my science officer Lieutenant Nishizawa last night. If we strip one of the tether cables out we'll have more then enough tubing for a hydroponic system."

"Do we have enough food seeds in storage?" Foley asks.

"We've got plenty of fruit and vegetables. But we're not going to be able to cultivate any grains though. They don't grow very well in hydroponics and there is no soil on the station."

"Those tethers are about 300 meters long," says Foley, "We should be able install it down the central corridors of the Ring with the recycling equipment in the middle."

"We've got to get it inside first," Fisher says.

"Maybe one of the hatches on the arms. They are about 100 meters long each."

"That might work. Of course you'll have to shut down one of the arms to get it in there."

"You've got an arm that's not operational over there don't you Commander?"

"I don't think there is enough internal space though."

"Yeah," Foley replies, "So Commander, do you think we

should explore the Gliese 581 system? Our scans so far show we could use a gravity assist from three planets on the way."

"Sounds like a good idea," says Fisher, "If we have to stay in orbit it will only require a small course adjustment. Any idea how long it will take to traverse the entire system?"

"Lieutenant Commander Singh says if we take advantage of the three assists, it would take about 9 months to move beyond the furthest planet's orbit," says Foley, "It would take about another 2 months to get to this system's asteroid belt. How are the repairs going?"

"It looks like the circuit breakers on the port side of the truss are fine. We'll reconnect them again and start powering up all of the equipment on that side of the truss. The SEV will be on autopilot today as we won't be able to power the external arms until the systems checkout," informs Fisher, "Once that is done I'll get engineering to look over the procedures and contact you."

"Sounds good station, Enterprise out."

"How are we looking Lieutenant?" asks Fisher over the intercom.

"It looks like we are getting power up to the radiator Commander," von Braun replies, "That's in line with the testing we conducted on the equipment a couple of days ago. If we can repair the pump we might be able to move the fluid through the piping but it won't be anywhere near full speed."

"What if you we're to cut back on the piping to the

damaged solar arrays? Would that give us some extra pressure?"

"Maybe Commander, but with the panels damaged there is no real need to keep it pumping at full capacity. Just enough to stop the pipes seizing up should do the trick."

"Have you had a chance to take a look at the procedure the Enterprise sent over?"

"I've been browsing over them all day and they look fine. I'm a bit concerned we don't have a direct anchor point and we'll be putting the tether around the core and ZeroG modules but we don't have much of a choice."

"Will we be able to handle the stress?"

"It should be fine. We'll be using two of the tethers connected together on the Enterprise's parabola frame. If the stress gets too much the connectors of the tethers will come apart," replies von Braun, "We should close all the hatches between all the modules on the lower core just in case something does happen and move the crew away from those sections."

"Good idea Lieutenant," replies Fisher.

All of a sudden a scratching noise can be heard for a couple of seconds. Fisher gets up and walks out of his ready room and into Ops.

"What has that?" Fisher asks.

"That was the seal on the connection module Commander," Ensign Dumas replies from the operations console, "Our rotation is beginning to dip below 2 RPM."

"How long till we reach critical rotation?" asks Chertok.

"A couple of days maximum," says Dumas, "If we don't get a boost soon we'll have to put the brakes on."

"Engineering, can we give the Ring the slightest of

boosts?" Fisher asks into his intercom.

"We just don't have enough power to generate enough of a reaction," von Braun replies, "All we could do now is just keep the current rotation constant but that's a waste of fuel."

"I'll talk to the Enterprise and see if we can get this connection happening," Fisher says, "My ready room Commander."

As the two enter the ready room, Fisher picks up a PAD and hands it to Chertok. The PAD, or Personal Access Device, allows for information to be shared without using any paper or limited resources.

"That's the crew list I've been working on for when we combine," says Fisher, "What do you think?"

"There are quite a few Enterprise personnel at the top of the list Commander," Chertok notes as he studies the crew positions.

"They know how to operate the ship. That's what they are trained to do," replies Fisher, "Besides, you'll be in charge of the Station Section."

Chertok smiles ever so slightly at the thought.

"Have you discussed this with Foley yet?" enquires Chertok.

"I was going to in a couple of days, but now we've only got those couple of days I think I'll send it over this afternoon."

"It would be a good idea to get it out of the way sooner," agrees Chertok, "Do you think we can connect the craft within two days?"

"Probably. If we need some extra time we can fire up the rotation engines for a few extra hours if needed. That won't waste too much fuel," says Fisher, "On your way out get comms to call Captain Foley and patch it straight through."

"Will do sir," says Chertok handing the PAD back.

Fisher studies it for a few seconds until Foley comes on the computer screen.

"This is a bit of a surprise Commander," says Foley, "What can I do for you?"

"It seems like everything Captain, our rotation is slowing down real fast," says Fisher, "The connector module is beginning to scrape against the core. We've only got a couple of days until we have to stop the rotation or it will start causing damage."

"You still don't want to consider the other options?" asks Foley.

"If the rotation stops we'll only have enough fuel to start it again. We won't have anything left to boost it over time," replies Fisher.

"Okay, I'll get our operations chiefs to coordinate manoeuvres and begin the docking," Foley says, "We'll also begin transferring the capsules over to the station. We'll wait until the docking is complete before transferring the Excalibur over. She's a bit bigger and will have to complete a longer trip."

"Thanks Captain. I really appreciate this."

Chapter Thirteen – Two become One

"5, 4, 3, 2, 1," Lieutenant Foster counts down.

"Ship Status," enquires Foley after a couple of seconds.

"All stations report no problems Captain," replies Ross.

"What is the status of the station?" asks Foley.

"Station reports no problems," says Foster.

"Notify the station we are clear as well," orders Foley, "I'm heading down to the core to meet the station crew. Commander you're with me. You have the conn Shipway."

As the two walk toward an Elevator through the ring, Ross notices that Foley is a bit quiet.

"You look anxious sir," says Ross.

"What, oh yeah," replies Foley, "Now the two are docked all it takes is a couple of words and Fisher can relieve me."

"I don't think he will do it quite that quickly sir."

"He send over a new crew assignment roster two days ago," says Foley, "If he isn't keen for the job I don't know what it is."

"Perhaps he was trying to help out."

"While he is still in command of the station, he had more pressing things to worry about other than crew rosters."

"Even so, we've been doing so much for them. He probably wanted to do something to get his mind off everything else."

"Maybe."

"So what are the new assignments, if you don't mind me asking,"

"Almost everyone stays where they are. He's the new Captain and commanding officer. Commander Chertok takes over operations on the station side. I become the ship's First Officer and you the Chief of Operations."

"So we're still separate?"

"I talked him into realising that everyone should continue doing their jobs. The Chief Engineers should continue to do their job, same with Operations. None of us know our respective spacecraft like ourselves."

The two enter the waiting elevator and strap themselves into their seats.

"Foley to Kōno, have our guests arrived yet?" Foley asks into the chairs intercom.

"The dock adapter is still pressurising Captain. It will take about another five minutes," Kōno replies.

"We are just coming up in the elevator now. We'll be there to open the hatch," says Foley closing the intercom.

"You ready for this Captain?" Ross asks.

"No time like the present," Foley replies tapping a button on his chair closing the elevator door.

Several minutes later the door to the elevator in the connection module opens.

"Welcome down to the dungeon Captain," Lieutenant Harrison says greeting the two command officers to the core.

"You do know how to put a smile on my face don't you Lieutenant," says Foley.

"I wanted the last time I call you Captain to be a good memory," chuckles Harrison.

Foley takes a deep breath.

"We'll let's do it," says Foley as he pulls up through the upper porthole.

After passing the core crew quarters they arrive in the

120

ZeroG Connection module. Then after righting himself to the 'floor' he continues up the two European modules. Both modules are the contribution from the European Space Agency. The first module is a medical experiment module containing some isolation chambers with various sensors as well as some of the ships medical supplies. The outer module was a flexible racking module where racks similar to computer server racks can mount equipment and storage compartments. Only about a third are full as the last supply shuttle was bringing the final equipment up with it.

Lieutenant Madison, ship's Head of ZeroG Science, is waiting with Lieutenant Kōno at the far end of the module.

"Captain, they are ready on the other side," says Kōno as Foley approaches the hatch.

After steadying himself, with a final glance to Ross, he nods to Kōno.

Kōno turns the latch then turns upside down grabbing the bar used to anchor her feat seconds earlier and lifts the hatch revealing Commander Fisher who is oriented 90 degrees clockwise to the Enterprise crew.

"If your going to command this ship Commander you'll want to learn which way is 'down'," says Foley with a big smile on his face. Fisher floats through the hatch before righting himself.

"Permission to come aboard Captain," Fisher asks.

"As long as you're not here to take my job," Foley replies much more seriously.

"Not quite yet Captain, there is still a bit of work to do," says Fisher.

"Permission Granted," says Foley.

"We need that power link up now," Fisher says with urgency, "Our rotation is down to 1.8 RPM. I'm surprised the docking didn't knock it down a little further."

"We've got the cables ready to go here Commander," Kōno says.

"von Braun will help you hook them up," says Fisher, "I'll get out of your way Lieutenant."

Commander Fisher moves out of the way as Kōno floats through the hatch trailing a power cable behind her.

"We've still got time if you want to change your mind on this Commander," says Foley, "Keeping the station basically tied to the ship is very risky."

"The station still has plenty to offer Captain," Fisher says.

"Alright. I want to show you something," says Foley as he floats back into the ship.

The two commanders continue straight through the core into the opposite modules.

"Take a look out here," says Foley as he pushes off the floor moving up into a dome.

Outside the SEV is preparing the tether cables with one end in a forward clamp near the edge of the shield frame.

"That is all that will be holding the two craft together," says Foley as he hands Fisher a pair of binoculars, "That frame, while designed to handle the impact of micro-asteroids, is only 40 centimetres thick. It's not even solid."

"You're still trying to talk me out of this?" asks Fisher.

"Well that," Foley replies, "and to show you how we are going to attach the cable. The frame is two rails connected by regular crossbeams about 40 metres apart. We will thread the two sides of the tether across one of those

122

crossbeams each before attaching the ends together. It will give us a slightly stronger bond between the two ends."

"Good idea," remarks Fisher while still looking through the binoculars, though now looking at the station, "I have seen the damage through the cameras but there is nothing like seeing it with your own eyes."

"That flare really did a number on your solar arrays didn't it," says Foley.

"We think it happened after that anomaly hit us," says Fisher, "We were still getting power through the arrays even with the shields down."

"I wish I knew what happened to us, what brought us all the way out here," remarks Foley.

"Whatever it was I think it's long gone," responds Fisher lowering the binoculars, "I wonder what's happening at home?"

"I don't want to think about that."

"You think they might have come to reality that we aren't there?"

"It's been more than 5 days. I think they would realise by now that we aren't in Earth orbit."

"Let's hope the shuttle and escape pods were able to make it out before that anomaly hit," says Fisher.

"I think two of them would have had a head start," Foley says looking out the dome, "They certainly aren't out here with us."

The two commanders look outside the dome, Foley looking toward Orion and Earth.

"I better get back to the station Captain, we've still got a few things to do before we can officially become one craft," Fisher says.

"Airlock to engineering, we have closed the hatch," says Ensign Paton.

"Thank you Ensign," replies von Braun, "Engineering to Commander Fisher, we are ready for you."

"I'm on my way Lieutenant," replies Fisher over the intercom.

For the safety of the crew, everyone has been moved to the core section of the station with all major operations being conducted from the engineering module.

"Engineering to Parry, did you get everything connected out there?" asks von Braun over the intercom.

"We sure did," say Parry in an overly confident voice, "I'd say this walk has been the better of them since we came out here."

"Very good," replies von Braun as Fisher floats into Engineering, "The attachment of the two ZeroG module is complete sir. We'll be ready to begin combined operations once the links are checked."

"Very good Lieutenant," Fisher replies, "Is the electrical link stable?"

"Yes sir, we've routed power into the Ring and the rotation engines are ready to be deployed."

"Okay Lieutenant. Ops, begin the deployment of the rotation engines."

"Aye sir," says Lieutenant Rawat from another console in Engineering.

At two opposite modules on the Ring, the engines emerge. No larger than an old space shuttle main engine, these

124

plasma pulse pods are designed to provide both the initial rotation and any required boost to maintain it. The pods are offset from the centreline of the modules they emerge from to provide a greater directional thrust. Within each of the modules is the fuel chamber and electrical systems.

"The pods are extended and fall back latches are in place Commander," informs Rawat.

"Okay, get the Enterprise on the line Lieutenant," orders Fisher.

"Enterprise here, go ahead," Foley responds.

"We are ready to begin rotation boost Captain. Everything good on your side?" asks Fisher.

"We've reduced our power requirements over here, you can go ahead at any time Commander," replies Foley.

"When you're ready von Braun," Fisher says.

"The engines are at optimal pre-fire temperature," says von Braun, "Activate engines."

The image on the display in engineering shows a slight yellow glows coming from the pods.

"We have a good engine sync," says Rawat.

"Increase thrust to 50%," orders von Braun.

The Ring on the screen begins to slightly move faster.

"Rotation speed has increased to 4.2 metres per second," informs Rawat.

"We're going to need a bigger push then that," says Fisher.

"How's the electrical systems over there Enterprise?" asks von Braun.

"We are stable over here Lieutenant. You can increase at anytime," says Kōno.

"Okay, lets increase to 70%," orders von Braun.

"Rotation is approaching 4.7 metres per second," says

Rawat.

"Is the Ring stable?" asks von Braun.

"No unexpected vibrations Lieutenant," replies Rawat.

"Electrical systems and fuel flow are stable, we could push it up to full Commander," informs von Braun.

"Lets do it," says Fisher.

"Bring it up to full Lieutenant," orders von Braun.

The exhaust on the pods begins to extend longer as the engines are pushed up to full power.

"Rotation is at 5 metres, full rotation in about one minute," says Rawat.

The Ring begins to make a noise on the connection module. Fisher looks at von Braun with a hint of concern.

"Don't worry sir, the RCS engines on the Ring are adjusting," reassures von Braun, "It always happens as the pods are not on opposite sides of the modules."

"You think they would have thought of that before building her," says Fisher.

"They did fix it for the Enterprise," responds von Braun.

"Rotation is a 5.6, 5.7, 5.75, 5.8, 5.85," says Rawat.

"Cut the engines," orders von Braun.

"Engines offline," informs Rawat, "Rotation holding steady at 5.9 metres per second, 2.52 rotations per minute."

"That's what I want to hear," says a happy Fisher.

"Engineering to all hands, no ops for 90 seconds," von Braun orders to ensure the station is running smoothly.

Everyone stops what they are doing, even some of the crew take advantage of the true no gravity and let go of their nearest railings.

In Earth orbit while astronauts experience weightlessness,

they are still feeling the effects of Earth's gravity but as a spacecraft is falling away at the same rate as the Earths curve, the experience is actually that of free falling. But gravity still affects things in orbit so crew still hold onto something to stop that effect from moving them too far. However with no nearby planet and the star in the distance no discernable gravity is felt on the now combined ship/station.

"No ops complete," von Braun says, "All stations report normal sir."

"Well then, it looks like we have gravity again," says Fisher, "Tell the Enterprise we are now ready to wrap the tethers around the station."

"Aye sir," replies Rawat.

"Begin activating the comm links through the ZeroG modules Lieutenant," orders Fisher moving to an intercom, "All personnel return to your normal stations."

Fisher leaves Engineering floating toward to connector porthole. Fisher moves through as the first of the returning crewmembers enter the module.

"Commander, a word," Fisher asks Chertok as they move to one side.

"von Braun is activating the links between the station and ship now," says Fisher taking a deep breath, "Now's as good a time as any. I'm heading over to the Enterprise. When you receive the notification of transfer of command you'll be in charge over here."

"Aye sir," says Chertok.

"We are going to have our night period once the tether is wrapped and if everything goes to plan we might attempt the first," says Fisher, "Make sure everyone is ready over here."

"Will do sir. When will the shuttle be transferred over?" asks Chertok.

"Probably in the morning. I'll contact you with the details. You have the conn commander."

"Aye sir. Good luck sir," says Chertok wishing the Commander fair well with a handshake.

"Hopefully with the change of luck today we might not need it," says Foley as he departs for the ship.

Chapter Fourteen – It's a Wrap

"Engineering to Ops, we are beginning to wrap the station," Kōno says over the intercom.

"Thank you Engineering," says Foley.

"Sir, Commander Fisher has arrived at the rear elevator shaft," informs Foster.

"You think this is it?" asks Ross.

"I can't think of any other reason why he would come all the way to the Ring," replies Foley as he begins to depart Ops, "Inform the module I'll be there in a few minutes."

As Foley moves through the modules leading to the elevator shaft, he can't help feel a sense of disappointment. Even though he has been the Enterprises commanding officer for the past few days, it still doesn't feel like he had the chance to be its true commander. All of the major operations occurred while still 'docked' in low Earth orbit. He didn't even get a chance to fire up the engines and set sail for the first time, the universe took care of that for him.

"Captain, Medical facilities are now fully operational," informs Lieutenant Liliya Pirogov, the Enterprises only dedicated medical officer.

"Thank you Lieutenant," responds Foley as he passes the infirmary continuing through an escape module.

Upon exiting the escape module, Foley spots Fisher entering the crew quarters.

"You are more keen than I thought," greets Foley.

"I didn't feel like waiting at the elevator," responds Fisher, "Besides, I think Ensign Li didn't either."

"I think the Ensign is itching to head up to Excalibur," says Foley, "I've assigned him to get some more experience in shuttle operations with Lieutenant Madison." The two commanders begin a slow stroll back to operations.

"It's been a long six days Captain," says Fisher.

"That it has," responds Foley.

"Who would have thought that humanities first extra-solar crew would be stuck in these metal cigar tubes?"

"Yeah, and so close to a star."

"What else have we found out about 581?"

"Commander Singh and Lieutenant Lenz have been conducting scans over the past few days," replies Foley, "They have been studying not only the star but also what they believe are the planets. So far everything look like our observations from Earth."

"How's our journey through the system going to pan out?" asks Fisher.

"It looks like we will miss most of the planets. We might meet up with 581g on the other side, but it looks like the other planets will be almost to our sides."

"You don't think there will be any chance to use the SEV?"

"Probably not. Unless we come upon a stray asteroid there really won't be an opportunity. We won't get close enough to 581g to conduct any SEV operations," says Foley.

"So, I think you know what's coming now," says Fisher after a few quite seconds.

"That I do," replies Foley.

"So how do you want to do it?" asks Fisher.

"By the book, as we are following it," responds Foley.

130

"Okay, by the book it is," says Fisher as they enter operations.

"Captain, Ensign Li has made it to the shuttle and they are ready to begin transfer operations," Foster informs Foley.

"Captain to Excalibur, your go for transfer operations," says Foley over the intercom.

"Aye Enterprise, depressurising airlock," replies Madison.

Fisher looks at Ross then Fisher and nods tapping the intercom for a ship wide broadcast.

"Attention crew this is Captain Foley. The past few days have been trying on our craft as much as ourselves. I have placed my full confidence in both our crews to get the job done, even under difficult circumstances and we have both proven we have what it takes, as they put it in an old movie, 'The Right Stuff'. But as we are now a united craft, we must also be a united crew. The regulations state that the most senior officer must take command that is unfortunately not me. So it is with pride, and a little regret, that I hereby transfer command of the Enterprise to Commander Fisher effective immediately. Commander, you have command."

"I relieve you commander," Fisher replies.

"I am relieved," says Foley.

"I don't know how I'm going to top that speech. We have had a difficult few days. But as each challenge has reared its ugly head, we have met it head on. While we continue as a united crew I expect we will meet each new challenge with the vigour and speed that we have over the past few days. Those days have been tough and we still have a long way to go before we can reach home. Let's never forget how we have come together and continue that spirit over the days and months to come. Good luck to our new Enterprise."

"Here here," says Foley.

"Here here," repeats the crew.

"Note in the ship's log the transfer of command," says Fisher.

"Aye Captain," replies Shipway.

"Well then Commander, let's do this."

"Aye sir," replies Foley.

"Distribute the new crew positions Shipway," orders Fisher.

"Transmitting to all stations now sir," says Shipway, and after a few moments replies, "All stations received sir."

"Firing RCS thrusters," says Ensign Li as the Excalibur comes to a stationary position off to the side of the station's core.

"Reading stationary Excalibur," Commander Parry informs over the radio.

"Begin plotting the rotation Ensign," Lieutenant Madison orders.

"Lieutenant, we should also begin the initial thrust moving the shuttle in line with the docking port," informs Li, "If we initialise thrust after the completing the rotation, the vented gas might affect the arm if it's directly above the shuttle."

"Good thinking Ensign, I'll get to it," Madison responds.

To offset any shift of the station when the Enterprise accelerates, the shuttle's engines will be pointed opposite the direction of travel to help boost the station. The acceleration of the ship will have to be timed to ensure the arms of the Enterprises Ring aren't below the shuttle's engines.

"Lieutenant, would we be able to angle the main engines so the exhaust misses the Ring?" Li asks, "It should also be able to provide a counter force to some rotation from the offset centre of gravity."

"Good thinking Ensign, I'll pass it onto Ops," responds Madison, "So I've run the simulations on the appropriate manoeuvres, we should be able to pull this off on auto-pilot. We will have to go out to 250 metres, then we can perform the manoeuvre to align the docking ports then push back in."

"Okay, I'll send the updated manoeuvres to the station team," says Li, "Do you really think this will work?"

"What, the shuttle assist?"

"No, moving both the ship and station."

"I wouldn't even be trying it if I was in charge," says Madison, "Too many risks, too much could go wrong."

"I'm worried about the shield," responds Li, "I don't think it can hold the station without causing any damage, and it is one of the critical components to travelling in space."

"Well our new Captain thinks it's worth the risk."

"I think he's grown attached to the station… no pun intended."

"I'm sure that Commander Foley has already discussed it with the Captain," says Madison, "We just have to support our command officers."

"Even if they are putting us at risk?" says Li.

"I trust Commander Foley to speak up if it gets that bad,"

responds Madison.

"I hope so, the last thing we need is anything else to go wrong out here," says Li.

"Excalibur, we are ready on the station for you to begin the manoeuvre," says Parry.

"Is the manoeuvre set in the auto pilot?" asks Madison.

"Course set Lieutenant," responds Li.

"Okay, let's do this," says Madison, "Activating thrusters." Madison taps a few buttons and the RCS thrusters in the nose vent gas, beginning the long trip out before rotation and docking.

The new setup of the ship is like some bizarre combination of two toy models. With the Enterprise facing forward, the ZeroG modules at the bottom of the station attached attached to the forward ZeroG modules on the ship. The station then extends down from the ship. If looking from the wrong angle one could mistake the two rings moving against each other, however with the station is offset 90 degrees, there is still a good 20 metres clearance between the two rings. The two craft look like a water main jutting off to different connections in different directions every what way.

As the Excalibur halts it's distancing, the SEV and several spacewalk team can be seen manipulating the tether around the station. The tether is first wrapped around one of the ZeroG modules a couple of times, then positioned under the Core and is now being wrapped around the opposite ZeroG module.

Moving back toward the station, Excalibur loses sight of the crew on the opposite side of the core. One might be able to call the docking a majestic dance in the sky, but with little to no movement beyond a direct approach to the docking port it feels little more than a train on its tracks moving closer to its inevitable destination.

"Okay station, notify the spacewalk crew we are ready for final approach," says Madison over the radio.

"Will do Excalibur," replies Parry.

A few second later, some of the team can be seen looking toward the shuttle, then securing themselves and their tools to the station. Even though the whole process will be automated, the last thing anybody wants is a bump from the core to fling them out into the true unknown.

"Station to Excalibur, the spacewalk crew are ready for you," radios Parry.

"You'd think the Captain would wait till they have finished before moving the shuttle," says Li.

"He does seem a bit too keen to get things done, but these are our orders," says Madison, "Station, synchronise the docking platforms."

As the two sides begin preparing for docking the two hatches come alive, activating lights and lasers to help guide the shuttle on to the station.

"Platform active," notifies Parry.

"Beginning alignment," says Madison as she presses a button.

At that moment, two lasers briefly become visible as they search for each other receiver. As the lasers focus and narrow they no longer become visible. The two systems begin talking to each other and the shuttle moves a few centimetres to port. Once the two hatches are aligned, the shuttle slowly approaches the station. The gap decreases from about 5 metres over a period of five minutes until the shuttles docking port is floating about 15 centimetres away from the stations. After a few stationary moments, the docking port from the shuttle extends out to the stations and captures the stations port. After the hard latches engage between the two docking ports, the shuttle pulls itself toward the station closing the previous 15 centimetre gap. Once the briefest of nudges occurs the shuttle is docked to the station.

"Excalibur to Enterprise, we are now captured. Begin no ops," says Madison over the radio.

Chapter Fifteen – Decent in the New Ranks

"How are you find Operations Commander?" asks Foley.

"Just like I remembered it sir," replies Ross from the operations console, "Though I've heard Commander Shipway isn't handling weightlessness very well in the core."

"It takes a bit of getting used to and not everyone can sail between sections as easily as us," says Foley, "How's the team doing outside?"

"They are returning the other end of the tether back to the shield frame. They should have the two ends secured within an hour," replies Ross, "How are you holding up sir?"

"Me."

"We weren't the only ones demoted today."

"Oh that. I'm handling it just fine, though I haven't done this much running around in space. The last time I was a First Officer was on a shuttle mission to repair a few satellites, and we didn't have any gravity to get sore legs in."

"It does take a while to get used to, though the Captain isn't spending much time moving around."

"He hasn't spent that much time out of his ready room at all," says Foley, "You think he might be planning a coup?"

"A coup, on his own ship. I don't think he would need too," replies Ross, "Besides, he's already the Captain, and no one around here is talking about mutiny… are you?"

"Me. No," chuckles Foley, "It's just he seems to want to

take things a little too quickly."

"Well unless he puts the ship in danger there's nothing you can do, at least by the regulations," says Ross.

"Regulations, you weren't keeping an eye on me were you Lieutenant Commander?" asks Foley with a look of not quite sincere doubt.

"Only doing my job sir," replies Ross with a smile on her face.

"Report on the tether Commander," asks Fisher as he exits the ready room.

"The team are bringing the other end back to the shield now sir. The attachment should be completed in an hour," replies Foley.

"Very good. Notify me when the procedure is complete. You have Ops Commander," says Fisher as he exits rearward.

"That was very brief," says Ross.

"Maybe. But he's the Captain, and what the Captain says goes," replies Foley.

"Sir, engineering is requesting we get ready for acceleration," says a slightly puzzled Lieutenant Foster.

"Ready for acceleration, that's not right. Put me through to engineering," asks Foley, "Engineering, confirm you want us to get the ship ready for acceleration?"

"Yes sir, those are my orders," responds Kōno.

"Orders, whose orders?" demands Foley.

"The Captain, he just contacted me from the infirmary," says Kōno.

138

"Shouldn't we test the engines first?" enquires Foley.

"I thought we could get a head start on the next few days," says Fisher as he enters Ops, "Besides, there's nothing like working under pressure to gauge how this new crew will get along."

"The engines are the one system we have yet to test. We performed the integration on thrusters only to save time," says Foley.

"Are you not going to carry out my orders Commander?" challenges Fisher.

"No sir," replies Foley, "Begin preparations for the acceleration Commander."

"Aye sir," replies Ross as she begins contacting the various departments.

"A word with you in my ready room Commander," Fisher asks Foley as he moves toward the ready room.

Foley and Ross exchange a concerning glance before Foley follows the Captain.

Foley enters the ready room as Fisher takes his seat.

"Now you've been a Captain yourself, how would you have liked it if your first officer questions you?" asks Fisher.

"Not much sir," replies Foley.

"Then if you have concerns there are appropriate times to raise them with me and in front of the crew isn't one of them. Is that understood?" chides Fisher.

"Yes sir," replies Foley, who asks after a few seconds asks, "May I speak freely sir."

Fisher nods his head.

"I understand you didn't like what I said in front of the crew but you put me in this position for a reason," says

Foley, "You kept me as first officer because I know the operations of this ship like… like its Captain."

"I'll take it you're coming to a point," says Fisher.

"Sir, there's a reason why I put in place the testing schedule on the engines. We don't know exactly what the conditions of the engines are after going through that anomaly. We need to conduct a full examination of the engines and their systems before we even think about moving the ship."

"Do you have any indications that the engines were damaged?"

"Nothing yet sir, but we still haven't conducted any tests yet unlike on almost every other system on the ship."

"I asked the SEV to swing by the engines on the way back," says Fisher, "They haven't reported and exterior damage."

"Sir, with all due respect. When did you order that?" asks Foley.

"Just before they completed the work on the tether," says Fisher.

"Why didn't I hear anything about this?" enquires Foley with a hint of annoyance.

"I asked Chertok to handle it," replies Fisher, "You guys were busy with the team and I didn't want to intrude."

"Chertok. Sir, Commander Chertok is in charge of the station section. As the First Officer of this ship I need to know of any additional operations, especially considering the SEV is assigned to the Enterprise," says Foley.

"Your right Commander," concedes Fisher, "In the future I'll run it past you."

"What did Kōno say about this?" asks Foley, "Surely she

140

would agree with you."

"She responded just like you," says Fisher, "But with a clear visual inspection, any problems with the systems will be picked up during engine activation and the engines will shut themselves down."

"Well all I can say is its risky sir. Without a full test we won't know of any of the unidentifiable problems until they arise," says Foley.

"Which Kōno says can be addressed as they occur," reassures Fisher, "Don't worry Commander, I've been going over this all day."

"A little head up next time would be better sir," says Foley.

"Are you still speaking freely Commander?" chides Fisher.

"Lieutenant, fuel transfer system flow test complete. Fuel is flowing between the fuel pods at the standard rate," informs Ensign Smith.

The Enterprise is fitted with 24 fuel pods arranged below the ring in the engine section at the bottom of the Core. Eight of the pods are arranged in a circle around the fuel injectors behind the engines providing fuel for immediate thrust. The injectors and the combustion chambers can be accessed from inside the ship in the Lower Engine module. Above the Lower Engine module is a general storage module. The next module, the Upper Engineering Module contains the internal systems for the engines, with the remaining 16 fuel pods arranged on the outside of the module. Above the Upper Engine Module is a module designed to hold a fusion reactor, however the systems were abandoned at the last minute leaving an empty module.

"Thanks Smith, are the pre-fire chamber heaters ready?" asks Kōno.

"Yes Lieutenant, heaters are responding to commands," replies Ross, "Current temperatures are about 120 Kelvin across the board."

"OK, activate the heaters at about 60%," orders Kōno, "once the chambers reach 350 Kelvin, increase to 100% until they reach 800 then maintain that temperature."

"Transferring coolant stream to the heaters," informs Ross, beginning the heater activation procedure by recycling the heat from the coolant system before they cycle to the radiators.

"Fisher to Engineering, how is the engine start-up sequence going?" Fisher radios from Ops.

"The electrics and fuel transfer systems check out Captain, we are beginning the pre-fire sequence on the engines now," replies Kōno.

"How long till they are ready for use Lieutenant?" asks Fisher.

"About 90 minutes Captain, but I must still stress we need to do more tests," urges Ross, "These engines have never been fire before in space. Our normal procedure it to test each engine..."

"We've already discussed this Lieutenant," interrupts Fisher, "you'll be able to handle any problems that occur when they show up, especially with the extra staff you've got from the station,"

"But sir-"

"My orders are clear Lieutenant."

"Yes sir," says Kōno.

"Are you still sure you want to go ahead with this Captain?" asks Foley in Ops, "The entire ships crew think its a bad idea, even if we can 'handle any problems when they occur'."

"Why wait for tomorrow when we can do it today?" asks Fisher rhetorically, "The sooner we can leave, the alone we get home."

"Don't forget sir, it won't be us getting home."

"Well the sooner our children, or grandchildren get home," says Fisher, "There's no use sitting around here doing nothing."

"You need to scratch it."

"Scratch what?"

"That itch sir, the one to get out there. To travel and explore."

"What makes you think it's that, Commander."

"It's the reason why I got this job in the first place," says Foley, "I want to get out there, but I also realise we need to take things slow, make sure things work and we can actually accomplish the goals that were given."

"Well, those goals have changed," says Fisher retreating to the ready room, "Our goal is to get home, anything else along the way is a bonus."

Chapter Sixteen – Captain's Orders

"Ops to all stations, begin lockdown for acceleration," orders Foley over the intercom.

All over the ship the crew begin closing supports, doors and hatches. Activity is a buzz like an old warship or submarine going into battle. If something does go wrong, the last thing the crew needs is a potential decompression spreading throughout this entire ship or supplies being flung every which way in zero gravity.

As rooms are checked and doors closed, a switch is thrown on each module indicating its readiness in Ops. Looking as the master display of the ships systems each module changes colour from orange to green, though that luxury isn't available for the station section that has to report in over the intercom.

"Chertok to Ops we are 50% green," the Commander notifies over the intercom, "Estimate six minutes till all green on station section."

"Hatches are stowed and hard latches are active on all attached spacecraft," informs Ross from the operations console, "Elevators are at their stations to ring side and inter-ship communications are normal."

"RCS thrusters are oriented for structural support during acceleration," says von Braun.

"Chertok to Ops, we've diverted additional power to the Core rotation module to reinforce and stabilise the seal for lateral acceleration, we are 70% Green."

"Infirmary to ops, we're ready for anything over here," radios Lieutenant Pirogov.

"Ring reports Green, Core 80% ready," says Ross.

"Engineering ready sir," informs Kōno, "but I must stress I'm not signing off on this sir, we absolutely need to conduct a test of the engines."

"I understand that Lieutenant, but you know the captains position on this," says Foley, "Singh, how's that course going."

"I've plotted a navigation program that will take us through the star system. We'll need to conduct some adjustment manoeuvres along the way but we should obtain a gravity assist from 581b in about 8 months on approach to the star," replies Lieutenant Commander Singh.

"Very good, transfer the course to the helm," orders Foley who taps the intercom, "Captain to the Bridge."

"Chertok to Ops, we are 100% green and ready for acceleration."

"Acknowledged station," says Foley as the Captain enters ops.

"How's our course looking?" asks Fisher.

"Commander Singh has plotted a course that will take us close to 581b for a gravity assist," informs Foley, "It's not a straight line to Earth now but once we exit the planets gravity we'll be pointed in the right direction."

"Course programed into the navigation computers Captain," Lieutenant Madison informs the Captain from the helm.

"Captain, we are 100% ready sir but Engineering is refusing to signal Green," informs Ross.

Captain Fisher looks at the Master Systems Display showing all bar the engines as green. Fisher reaches for the intercom.

"You know Lieutenant Kōno's stand on this sir as well as mine," interrupts Foley, "She want's it on the record and it's her way of showing it."

"Is there going to be a problem with it Commander?" asks Fisher.

"No sir, the engines are ready as they can be," replies Foley, "But I still have my doubts about their readiness."

"You know my stance?" Fisher quietly enquires.

"Yes sir, that's why I've signed off on it," says Foley continuing, "but with a protest in the ships log."

Fisher moves to the centre of Ops, takes his seat in the Captain's chair and taps the intercom for a ship wide broadcast.

"Attention crew of the Enterprise. I know the past week or so has been tough on all of us, but it's time to move forward, and head home. Our course will take us around Gliese 581b for a gravity assist and when we emerge we will be on our way home. I know some of you have concerns we might be moving too fast, but I have faith in this crew to react to any challenges that may be thrown our way with the speed and expertise that your training has instilled in each and every one of you. Let's go home people," finishes Fisher as he closes the ship wide intercom, "Helm, set course on programmed path."

"Aye sir," replies Madison.

"Engineering, set thrust program to 80%," orders Fisher.

"80% aye," replies an unconfident Kōno.

"All hands, prepare for acceleration in 10 seconds," notifies Fisher over the intercom.

"Engines at my command," says Madison.

"Engage" orders Fisher.

"Acceleration in 3, 2, 1, Mark."

A large jolt shakes Ops as the entire ship accelerates forward. However the acceleration continues at an alarming rate. The entire ship starts shaking violently as the acceleration increases much higher than the ships designed specification. A bright light comes from the rear of the ship as it moves forward at an alarming speed. A speed so fast and unexpected the station begins to move back toward to ship. An explosion is felt from the rear of the ship as an engine overloads causing an even larger jolt of speed to the ship.

Sparks begin flying around ops as the crew begin to regain their senses.

"Velocity is currently 1000 metres per second and increasing sir," notifies Madison from the helm. Acceleration at 5G and rising."

"That's not right," says a winded Fisher, "We should only be moving a few meters per second."

Another jolt is felt throughout the ship.

"Engineering to Ops, we've lost two engine-" the intercom cuts out on Kōno.

"What the hell's happening?" says Fisher.

"Two engines are out sir," informs Singh, "We are loosing structural integrity in the core section.

"Li to Ops, we need to cut the engines now as the station is moving toward the ship at an alarming rate," Li radios from his station at an elevator shaft.

"Ops to Engineering. Cut engines, I repeat cut engines," says Fisher into the intercom.

ACT THREE

Chapter Seventeen – What the…

"The intercom to the Core is down sir," informs Ross.

"Then inform them however you can," says Fisher as the vibrations and acceleration begin to slow.

"Acceleration slowing, reading 5G's, 4G's," informs Singh.

"Looks like they got the message sir," says Foley as he stands up after being flung across the room.

"Acceleration returning to normal sir," says Singh as a large explosion shakes the ship.

"How's the station Li," ask Fisher.

"It's still moving toward us," informs Li, "I recommend we match its rotation."

"The capsules and shuttle are on the station and they should be able to arrest some of their rotation," informs Madison, "I'm rerouting our RCS thrusters to match the station rotation."

"Make it quick Lieutenant," orders Fisher as Madison begins sending commands to the systems, "Report on our system status."

"Comms with the Core section are still down sir as well as the station section," replies Ross.

"Structural integrity and upper core systems look fine sir," says Foley looking at the Master Systems Display, "the Ring is rotating at about 0.92G's, but the lower core around the engine section is showing red, though we've still got power coming from the truss."

"Radio signal coming in from the station section sir," says Ross.

"Patch it through," says Fisher.

"Ops, this is von Braun in station Engineering."

"Go ahead. What's your status over there?" asks Fisher.

"Not good sir. We've got hull breaches in the ZeroG modules connecting to the ship. Comms are also down to the Ring over here and I can't raise Chertok."

"We've matched rotation with the station section Captain," informs Madison.

"What are the systems like over there?" asks Fisher.

"Not good, the lines look like they are severed through the ZeroG modules and we're not getting any power from the truss. Life support seems to be stable so far but the Rotation module is scraping pretty bad. I'd say it's misaligned and slowing down. I'll get back to you when I've got more information on the other systems."

"I've got comms back with the Core sir," informs Ross.

"Engineering, what's the status of the Core up there?" enquires Fisher.

"Not good Captain," replies Kōno, "the upper core is fine however the fire doors to lower engineering are sealed."

"Can you open them?"

"No Captain, there must be a containment breach in one of the engine systems. I know we've either lost some engines or they have sustained heavy damage. I shut them down as soon as I could but we were flung all over the place."

"Are there any crew in there?"

"Yes sir, Lieutenant's Harrison and Rawat were monitoring the fuel flow and engine temperatures."

"Do you know if they are alright?"

"Unknown sir, but if there was a containment breach…"

Kōno pauses.

"Understood, I'm sending Li, Pirogov and Madison down to help once they have cleared a path too one of the elevator arms," informs Fisher, "Let me know when you know more."

"Aye sir," replies Kōno.

"Ensign Li and Lieutenant Pirogov head to the Core section clearing modules on your way, you too Madison," orders Fisher over the intercom.

"von Braun to Ops, I've managed to open a comm line to Ops on the station but no one's answering. I can also confirm that ZeroG modules Columbus and Cook have lost life support and have been breached. I've also inspected the ZeroG connector module and it's bent out of shape where the cable wraps around it. It's sealed off for now but its life support systems are still functioning."

"Anyone trapped in those modules Lieutenant?" asks Fisher.

"Lieutenant Jackson and Ensign Al Majid are in the connection module and are communicating through the hatch, but Ensign Dumas was in Cook and they haven't heard anything from Him."

Fisher pauses with a look of regret on his face. Foley places a hand on his shoulder to comfort the Captain. Fisher composes himself.

"When it's safe get those two out," says Fisher, "If they haven't heard from Dumas by then we'll try to get him from our side."

"Aye sir."

"Station to Ops, this is Ensign Walsh, I'm in Ops over here," radios Walsh.

"Ensign, how are things there?" says Fisher.

"Ensign Paton and Commander Chertok are dead sir," informs Walsh as Fisher sinks into his chair, "they both suffered blunt force trauma from a panel that collapsed. There's nothing I can do sir."

Fisher slumps in his chair, head in hands.

"Sir?" enquires Walsh over the radio.

"Continue clearing the modules around the Ring over their Ensign," says Foley, giving Fisher a chance to compose himself, "Once finished report to von Braun in the core."

"Aye Commander."

"Sir, if you need some time," offers Foley.

"No that won't be necessary... actually, arrange for repairs to begin on the ship and," pauses Fisher recomposing himself, "reactivate the transport pod. If we can't get straight over there through the ZeroG modules-"

"Don't worry Captain, I'll look after it," says Foley as Fisher retreats to the Ready Room.

Chapter Eighteen – You're the Man!

"I've got power to the internal sensors," informs Ensign Li working from a panel between the Engineering modules.

"Hook them up to the portable terminal," orders Kōno, "We need to know what conditions are like in there."

"Here are the environment suits," says Lieutenant Pirogov floating into the upper engineering section, "I'll head back up to the medical bay and grab some supplies. Any indications from inside yet?"

"Not even a tap Lieutenant," says Kōno as Pirogov pivots and begins moving back up the Core.

"I've got environmental sensors active," says Li.

"What's it like in there?" asks Kōno.

"They are taking samples now," informs Li, "Reporting high levels of carbon, carbon dioxide, some fluoro-polymers."

"What about air?"

"Very low oxygen levels, certainly not enough to breath. There are also a few other chemicals that are reporting as unknown but the internal sensors are too sophisticated. The pressure is also quite low, about half an atmosphere."

"Take some samples and I'll get a portable analyser sent down from one of the science modules."

"I've cleared the docking hatch," says Lieutenant Lenz floating into Engineering, "Though the intercom is down on A and B ZeroG platforms."

"I'll let ops know, can you retrieve a portable gas analyser from one of the ZeroG science platforms for us Lieutenant," orders Kōno.

"Kōno to ops, we've got limited power to the lower engineering modules but we'll need to analyse the atmosphere in there before we can go in."

"Thanks Lieutenant, how long will it take?" replies Foley.

"About half an hour until we analyse the first samples, but there's still a few hours before we can vent the module then open the hatch," says Kōno, "Lenz informs me the docking hatch for the transport is cleared for use."

"I'll notify the station. What do you think the status of lower engineering is?"

"All indications show a breach and explosion somewhere in the engine links. If that's the case anyone in there had no chance," replies Kōno.

"Thank you Lieutenant, report back when you know more. Ops out," says Foley.

"Station to Ops, we've verified integrity of the ZeroG central module," radios von Braun, "We are ready to begin retrieval operations of the two crewmembers."

"Proceed with caution Lieutenant, we don't want to lose anymore resources over there," says Foley, "Have you heard anything from Parry in the shuttle yet?"

"No sir, I can't raise him," replies von Braun.

"We'll try a remote link from the ship here, Ops out," says Foley, "Shipway, attempt to establish a remote link with the shuttle and find out how Parry is going."

"Yes sir but I'm not that familiar with the shuttles systems," replies Shipway.

"I'll help you out," offers Foster, "After all I did pilot it up here."

"Very good Lieutenant, inform me when you've got the link," orders Foley who returns to his console, shifting through camera images of the engines.

"Are they the latest images from the SEV?" enquires Ross from the neighbouring console.

"Yeah, It looks like we've got damage to the emitters on engines 3 and 5," says Foley, "It also looks like an explosion behind engine 6. Singh, have you plotted our current course?"

"Looks like we are travelling about 2 degree to starboard compared to our original course Commander," Singh replies.

"What about our velocity?"

"We're traveling at about 17000 kilometres per hour or 4500 metres per second."

"How long were those engines active?" Foley enquires.

"About 12 seconds," replies Singh.

"That's almost three miles a second," says Ross.

"We should have only achieved a velocity of about 100 metres per second after a 10 seconds thrust," says Singh.

"I've got a feeling what ever happened was something to do with the fuel," speculates Foley.

"Not the engines?" enquires Ross.

"Well they are certainly damaged," says Foley looking at images of the damaged engines, "But you'd need to blow an entire fuel cell to produce enough thrust to get anywhere near that type of velocity and they all look fine in the inspection."

"I don't think the captain is holding up very well," says Ross looking toward the Ready Room.

"He's just lost more crew members on top of those we lost when we got here," says Foley, "I'd feel the same way if it were me."

"He hasn't come out of there since going in a couple of hours ago," mentions Ross.

"I'll go deliver another report," says Foley getting up from the console, steadying himself in the slightly reduced gravity, "I'll try and cheer him up."

As Commander Foley enters the Captain's Ready Room, he notices Fisher staring out the window and the opened bottle of rum on the desk.

"Sir, I thought I'd give you an update," says Foley.

"What's the latest Commander?" responds Fisher, his gaze not leaving the stars outside.

"The SEV has completed another pass of lower engineering and the engines. Engines 3 and 5 took heavy damage and the breach looks like it occurred behind engine 6."

"The pre-fire chamber?"

"Possibly, though it could have come from the fuel line as well."

"Have they got into lower engineering yet?"

"They are taking air samples now but indications are no survivors."

Fisher lowers his head, looking at his drink.

"Looks like I can't get any luck around here," says Fisher.

"Well what ever happened has accelerated us up to about 17000 kilometres per hour, we'll be passing the centre of Gliese 581 in about 6 months," replies Foley.

"And the station?"

"They are attempting a retrieval of the crew in the ZeroG

central module as we speak though they should be fine," says Foley, "We're attempting a remote link to the shuttle now to see how Lieutenant Parry is. It should be up anytime now."

"I should have listened to you guys," says Fisher turning his gaze to the Gliese 581 star just rotating into view, "You gave me plenty of warning."

"Now's not the time sir."

"No, you were right. I should have scratched that itch like you said."

"We couldn't have known this would happen."

"But it has."

"We shouldn't be second guessing ourselves, at least until we know exactly what caused the damage."

"Well it wasn't a meteor shower as the radar was clear and we're not in an asteroid belt," says Fisher, "And the engines checked out with the pre-flight SEV inspection."

"Stop beating yourself up over it Captain," reassures Foley, "There's still dozens of things that could have gone wrong, and we won't know till we get in lower engineering."

"But still, more dead under my command," says Fisher.

Foley begins to respond but is interrupted by the door chime.

"Yes," says Fisher as the door opens and Ross enters the ready room.

"We've got the remote link to the shuttle active," informs Ross.

"How is Parry?" asks Foley.

"That's why I came in here," says Ross as Fisher lowers his head again, "We've checked both the visible and infrared camera's. Lieutenant Parry is dead."

"Any idea how?" asks Fisher.

"There are several panels on the shuttle that have come loose and Parry has a wound to his head," says Ross.

The three stand in silence for a few seconds before Foley speaks up,

"Tell the station to get Walsh in there, just in case," orders Foley, "I'll note it in the ships log. That will be all Commander."

Ross nods and leaves the room.

"I was going to request Parry become the stations first officer when Chertok returned to Earth in a few weeks," says Fisher.

"He certainly proved over the past week that he's a real multi-tasker," says Foley, noticing the rum bottle on the desk is still full.

"That he was, a real all rounder," says Fisher, "You had your eyes on Lieutenant Harrison didn't you?"

"A fine Engineer certainly," responds Foley, "If he kept up his performance I was going to recommend him for the Chief Engineer position of this ships first flight with Kōno retiring after this mission."

"You two we're quite the pool player I hear?" asks Fisher, turning around for the first time.

"Yeah, I was even think of rigging up a pool table out of the spare supplies," says Foley with a smile, "He even joked about the Core being the dungeon that last time I saw him."

"Yeah he did have a sense of humour," says Fisher, "That was just before I came over and took command wasn't it.

"Yes sir."

"Well, it's good you came in when you did. I didn't want to

be drunk giving my last order as Captain," says Fisher.

"Sir?" enquires Foley with a look of confusion.

"I've been thinking about it since coming in here," says Fisher, "I didn't listen to any of your warnings, even when the Chief Engineer stressed to me we should have used the engines."

"As I said sir, now's not the time for second guessing-"

"But it is. We need the best people to repair this ship and that person isn't me. I couldn't even let the station go and look at the live lost because of that decision."

"Sir you should think this over."

"I've been thinking it over for the past few hours. While I've certainly got seniority, I have neither the training nor experience for this role. I didn't even take a sip of this rum when coming to this decision, and you know how much I like rum," says Fisher showing the seriousness of his decision, "We need the most experience and knowledge now more than ever."

"I don't know what to say," responds Foley.

"Well I'll say it for you. Congratulations Captain," says Fisher holding his hand out.

"I relieve you Captain," says Foley accepting and shaking Fishers hand.

"I am relieved," Fisher not only says but also expresses, then taps the intercom, "Lieutenant Commander Ross, note in the ships log I have surrendered command of the Enterprise to Captain Fisher."

"Sir?" enquires Ross.

"Those are my orders commander," responds Fisher.

"Aye sir."

"Well then, the ship and ready room is yours Captain,"

says Fisher finally sculling the glass of rum and starts leaving the ready room.

"Not so fast Commander," says Foley, "We've got our ship to repair, and the least I can afford you is the same as what you did for me. I need my first officer to have experience with the station just like you did with this ship."

"Thank you sir," says Commander Fisher.

"Now, lets get us up and running again," says Captain Foley.

Chapter Nineteen – How Bad?

"There, your suit is sealed," says Pirogov as she tapes over the final seal on Lieutenant Kōno's Environment Suit.

"Thanks Lieutenant," says Kōno tapping a panel on her wrist, "Beginning seal tests."

The environment suit is designed similar to an expedition suit, though it's primarily used within spacecraft. Each suit can be hooked up to oxygen supply lines to ensure an appropriate breathing environment, though they lack pressure and radiation protection of the expedition suits.

"The pressure inside lower engineering has stabilised at one atmosphere," informs Pirogov silencing an alarm on the hatch between the two modules, "Air filtration complete."

"My suit is reporting sealed," says Kōno looking at the wrist panel, "Comm check with the storage module."

"We hear you Lieutenant," responds Ensign Li over the radio.

"Okay, lets begin by closing the hatch on upper engineering," says Kōno as the two suited astronauts float up to the top of the module.

"Make way Lieutenant, I'm coming down with you," says Foley as he floats through the hatch.

"That's not necessary Captain," says Kōno.

"I know Lieutenant, but I'm down here in the Core so I may as well help out," replies Foley, "Besides, this suit needs an air out. It's not like I'll get a chance to use it again."

"If you wish Captain," says Kōno, "Help me close this

hatch."

Both Foley and Kōno place their feet in holsters in the 'floor' of the module and then begin closing the hatch from the 'roof'. Due to the damage the hatch needs to be closed manually. Once the hatch has been closed due to an emergency, the servos connected to the arms aren't considered a critical system until they are reconnected.

"Hatch closed. Check the seal Ensign," asks Kōno.

"Hatch depressurising now," informs Li and then informs seconds later, "Hatch is now sealed."

"Okay, seen as you're both here, we'll open both sides of the emergency door at the same time," says Kōno as they float to the other side of the module.

"You really are putting me too work," says Foley.

"Captain, Lieutenant. Take these spanners and insert them into the door cogs just here," instructs Kōno, "Make sure they are seated into the turning bolt. When instructed, turn the spanner half a rotation clockwise. I'll be here to insert these struts to keep the doors open with each turn."

As Foley and Pirogov position themselves, Kōno retrieves the struts from a storage compartment at the bottom of the door. Each support is 10 centimetres in length and slot into the door jam to keep the force-loaded door open until it is unlocked.

"We will need to complete 8 full rotations to unlock the door, it can then be moved freely," informs Kōno as she gets into position.

"Okay, make the first rotation," orders Kōno.

With the rotation of the spanners, the doors begin moving apart. The half rotation creates a gap in the door of about 10 centimetres.

166

"Do either of you feel any resistance?" asks Kōno as she places the first support into the door jam.

"No, it feels smooth enough," says Foley as Pirogov shakes her head.

"If any of you feel any resistance, let us know then let the doors return to their previous position," informs Kōno, "Let's make the next rotation."

The three astronauts work for 10 minutes to open the door, peering into the dark module during the short breaks.

"Okay, this is the final rotation," informs Kōno, "At about 120 degrees, you'll feel some resistance. That's the lock. Push past it and the doors will move freely."

"Okay Lieutenant, let's do this," say Foley as he and Pirogov make the final rotation. After two clunks, the doors jiggle and the spanners begin moving freely.

"That's it, they are unlocked," says Kōno as she moves up to the door and pushes one side into it's recess, Foley following suit with the other half.

Kōno then takes a torch from her belt and begins shining a light into the module.

Burnt consoles and panels can be seen all over the module, with several panels blown inward near the far end.

As the three astronauts enter and begin inspecting the damage, Kōno moves down the end to the exploded panels.

"Looks like the fuel injector overloaded, though the damage is contained to the inside of the module," says Kōno inspecting the gapping hole about 20 by 40 centimetres.

"How's the atmosphere in here Lieutenant?" asks Foley.

"It's breathable, but these walls will need a good scrub down once I can confirm it's safe to do so," responds Pirogov, "We don't want to be adding toxic dust to the station's air."

"We'll filter the air in upper engineering before opening the hatch up there," says Kōno continuing to inspect the damage, "It looks like the inner side of the outer hull is scorched but undamaged, though I do recommend welding a patch on the outside as a safe measure."

"Any damage to the other components?" asks Foley.

"They do have some scorching damage on the outside, though I'll have to inspect them after they are cleaned before testing them again," says Kōno.

Foley notices some threads in the top of the door jam. Upon pulling them out, he seas part of the ships patch.

"It would have been quick sir," say Pirogov, "At least that's what the damage indicates."

"Foley to Ross," radios the Captain.

"Yes sir," replies Ross.

"Note in the ships log Lieutenant's Harrison and Rawat are deceased," says Foley, "Pirogov will be making the official report later."

"Aye sir," says Ross.

The door to the transport pod opens and Commander Fisher emerges into the station. He looks around at the empty room and begins to realise the state of the station. Several panels are buckled, with one section of the chassis protruding into the module where the tether cable is wrapped around the station. With nobody to greet him, Fisher begins moving up the Core. When he emerges into the Rotation module he begins to feel disoriented.

"I put the breaks on the Ring sir," says von Braun from the Engineering module immediately above, "It was the only way to maintain a stable power connection out to the Ring."

"I've never seen it so still," comments Fisher, "Almost peaceful isn't it?"

"Thing's aren't good over here sir. It looks like we might have sustained structural damage to the starboard side of the trust. The radiator and coolant systems are working, but we're getting no energy from the solar arrays," informs von Braun as Fisher enters engineering.

"What about the other damage?" asks Fisher.

"From what I can tell we've got structural damage to the ZeroG Platform, particularly Platform D that is connected to the Enterprise. Platforms A and B are responding to diagnosis protocols but Platform C is on the same grid as D and those modules aren't responding. I've resealed the ZeroG Central module as a precaution."

"What about the Ring?"

"All the modules are reporting to diagnosis. There are no hull breaches, though a few panels loose and a bit of a clean up will be needed. We won't be able to use the elevators with no power, though as it's not rotating that isn't much of a problem at the moment."

"Will you be able to restart the rotation?"

"That core module was making some pretty bad noises. I think it's out of alignment. If there is any physical damage to the seal I don't think she will be moving for quite a long time. How's the Enterprise?" asks von Braun.

"It looks like a fuel injector overloaded and breached into lower engineering," says Fisher, "It's going to be one hell of a clean up over there."

"There was one thing I noticed," says von Braun, "During acceleration the emissions from the engines didn't look normal."

"How so Lieutenant?" enquires Fisher.

"Well sir, the engines usually emit a blue colour when they are operational," responds von Braun, "I also witnessed an explosion on one of the engines, it was green in colour."

"Green, what should an exploding engine look like?" asks Fisher.

"Well generally the materials and fuel would normally give off a white colour leading to the red spectrum, but this was definitely green," says von Braun.

"Any idea what could cause that?"

"It would have to be the fuel Commander, there's nothing else that could change the colour. Also given the velocity we achieved in such a short time it would have been something much more powerful than the normal fuel."

"Thank you Lieutenant, I'll pass it on," says Fisher, "I'm going to head up to the Ring."

"I could to with a spare hand from the ship. We've still got to check the other ZeroG modules," asks von Braun.

"You've got me Lieutenant, will that do?" responds Fisher.

"For now," says von Braun as Fisher exits engineering back into the rotation module.

Still feeling some disorientation from the lack of movement of the walls, Fisher takes a moment before heading for one of the elevator doors.

"Not that one sir," says Walsh, "that elevator became lodged in the shaft as the station moved. You'll have to go down here."

"Thanks Ensign," says Fisher floating over to the opposite side, "How are Lieutenant Jackson and Ensign Al Majid doing?"

"They were a bit shaken up but they did get a rest before we bought them back into the Core," replies Walsh as the two begin to traverse the elevator arm, "They are cleaning up throughout the Ring."

"I hope the damage wasn't too bad up here," says Fisher.

"Not quite sir, it's just loose panels and the like," says Walsh, "Structurally all the modules seem fine and sealed, though Ops was at the wrong part of the rotation cycle and felt the full brunt of the acceleration."

"Chertok and Paton?" enquires Fisher as the two emerge from the elevator arm and begin moving to Ops.

"I've moved them to the infirmary sir. Once everything's cleaned up over here I'll complete an autopsy."

"Have you done one before Ensign?"

"We watched a few in medical school, but I don't know how I'm going to complete one in weightlessness."

"I'll see if I can get them transferred to the Enterprise. It'll make the job a little easier."

As the two floats through the sleeping quarters module the other crewmembers can be seen tidying up each room, putting clothes into draws and returning mementos to shelves, securing them for the lack of gravity.

When Fisher emerges into Ops, damage is plain to see. Displays, panels and chairs having been dislodged now secured.

"This place was never designed for such acceleration," says Fisher looking around.

"Sir." enquires Walsh.

"The station was only designed for the odd orbital boost, nothing like the Enterprise let alone what we just experienced," says Fisher, replacing some mission patches on one of the walls, "I should have thought of that."

"As I said sir, it was also at the wrong part of its rotation. It was moving in the opposite direction to the ship. If it hadn't been for that there probably wouldn't be this much damage."

"Another thing to add to the tally that I did wrong."

"I wouldn't go that far sir, you couldn't have known-"

"Everyone keeps on saying that," interrupts Fisher, "More deaths under my watch."

"Well Foley did sign off on it didn't he?" says Walsh, "It wasn't like they mutinied, so you weren't that far off the mark… at the time."

"Have you completed an assessment of the damage yet?" asks Fisher.

"I've just sent this one down to von Braun," says Walsh handing Fisher the PAD.

"Are any of these consoles operational?" enquires Fisher.

"Those two over there are," says Walsh pointing close to the entry they just came through.

"Thank Ensign, you get back to the clean-up," says Fisher floating over to the consoles tapping the intercom, "Fisher to von Braun, do you have a damage assessment for me yet?"

"A preliminary one sir. I've included a repair schedule with it but I'll need to do some more external inspections," replies von Braun.

"Send it up to console 4B in Ops."

"On it's way Commander."

As the files opens, Fisher reads through the list of damaged systems, the severity of their damage and the possibility for repair or replacement.

"Ops to Station," radios Foley.

"Fisher here."

"How are things over there?"

"Not the best Captain, I'm going over the most recent damage assessment now. It looks like we've lost Columbus and possibly the Core ZeroG platform. Cook looks undamaged but we'll need the SEV to make closer inspections of the entire ship. The Solar systems are down and we're working on one radiator and coolant loop. The Ring has been stopped as there seems to be problems with the Rotation module. We can't get to the other ZeroG modules yet. Beyond that there are panels and consoles loose or detached all over the station. von Braun is conducting further diagnosis of the ZeroG platform and the rest of the crew are cleaning up over here. I'll send the report over."

"Thanks Commander," responds Foley, "The SEV is recharging over here. I'll send it over in about three hours."

"How's the clean up of lower engineering going?" asks Fisher.

"I'm heading down there now," says Foley, "The toxicity report of the burn residue has come back clear. That will make the clean up move along a little bit quicker. Once the clean up is finished, I'll send another crew member over there to assist you guys."

"Thanks Captain, we'll need it," says Fisher.

Chapter Twenty – That Bad

"All I wanted to do was air this suit out Lieutenant, not make it a permanent part of my uniform," says Foley climbing back into his environment suit.

"You won't need to tape over the seals this time but there are still some fine particles that we don't want you inhaling," says Pirogov.

"There you go Captain," says Li sealing the helmet onto the suit, "This is a pressure hatch Captain."

"I know what they are Ensign," says Foley.

"Just giving you a reminder Captain," says Li as Foley makes his way into the temporary pressure hatch.

The Pressure hatch is a flexible air sealed 'airlock' which has two zippered sides. As someone enters the 'clean' side there is no additional pressure being exerted. Once the zip is closed a fan is activated pushing more air into the hatch creating a positive air pressure. While the zipper to the 'dirty' side is open, the fan continues to push more clean air out of the hatch, preventing debris from entering. While not a completely airtight system, it's an adequate alternative where the environment is generally normal.

As Foley emerges through the other side of the pressure hatch noticing a much cleaner and brighter engineering.

"Kōno is checking the other engine systems," says Pirogov, resealing the pressure hatch.

Past two other crewmembers scrubbing panels, bulkheads and equipment is Lieutenant Kōno, her head stuck behind panels to the fuel transfer systems of each engine.

"How's it going down here Lieutenant," asks Foley.

"Well the firewalls stopped the fuel from the ruptured fuel line spreading forward to the pre-fire chambers or back into the fuel cells," says Kōno, her head still in the conduits, "The hull also looks to have escaped any exterior damage but I'll still get a plate put on the outside."

"What about the other conduits?"

"I've inspected the lines to engines 8, 7, 5 and I'm just looking at 4 now," says Kōno, "There's no external damage on the lines though these conduits on 5 and 7 are warped from the explosion and I'll have them replaced."

"What about the other engines?"

"I'm moving around to them now. There doesn't seem to be any damage to the pre-fire chambers of engines 3 and 5 so the damage must be isolated to the cover," says Kōno, "I'll need to do a complete inspection of the other engines."

"How long will that take?" asks Foley, swiping a flake of soot away from his helmet.

"It's going to be a complete inspection," says Kōno, "It's going to take 3 or 4 days for each engine."

"Each engine?" says Foley with a hint of disbelief.

"Each engine is going to need to be disassembled. It will take a good day to do that on each engine, then a further day to clean up and repair any damage detected by the SEV overnight, then if we are lucky only a day to put them back together," says Kōno floating down out of the narrowing module, "But I've got a feeling we won't need all our engines."

"Why to do you say that Lieutenant," says Foley as Kōno floats over to a case in the cleaned section.

"This is why," says Kōno opening the case and showing

176

the Captain a sealed vial filled with an unfamiliar liquid.

"What is it?" asks Foley taking the vile.

"That came out of the hydrogen fuel tank Captain, and I can tell you that's not hydrogen," says Kōno.

"Shouldn't hydrogen be a gas at room temperature?" enquires Foley.

"Exactly, not only that but it shouldn't have a colour to it and that is green," says Kōno, "We put a sample through the gas analyser but it can't identify it. We'll need to put it through molecular analysis to find out exactly what it is."

"Is all the fuel… contaminated?" asks Foley.

"Just the hydrogen tanks. I don't know if it was one before we tested the fuel transfer systems but all eight of them are like that now," replies Kōno as Foley looks to the walls, with the fuel cells attached just outside the walls of lower engineering, "Don't worry Captain, as far as I can tell it's stable."

"von Braun did report seeing a green colour being emitted from the engines and the resulting explosion," says Foley, "Ensure you check all the fuel pods, including the shuttle and capsules."

"Well without knowing exactly what it is I think we have our culprit," says Kōno.

"How long till you can begin inspecting the engines?" asks Foley.

"We'll spend the rest of today cleaning up and inspecting in here. I'll begin planning tomorrow and we can disassemble the first engine the day after," says Kōno.

"Very well Lieutenant, notify me when you've finished up here. I'm heading down to the Ring," says Foley as he begins floating back to the pressure hatch.

177

"Will do Captain."

To say the engines are impressive is an understatement. The HDTL's pre-fire chamber converts the gas fuel into plasma and the cover directs the path of ions that are repelled away from the engines ensuring a clean thrust with low energy waste. The cover has ducts that ions travel down to escape the pre-fire chamber and also contains additional electromagnetic generators to direct the thrust without having to move each engine.

In it's current state, Engine 5's cover is looking worse for wear.

"Engine 5 looks just like engine 3," says Kōno over the radio from her space suit, "There isn't any direct damage to the magnetic emitters on the outside but there is on the exhaust ducts."

"Is the damage as extensive as engine 3?" asks von Braun.

"Not quite," replies Kōno, "but there's no way to salvage this cover. There is a major crack all the way through quadrant 3 leading into 4. Have you got power to the cover motors yet?"

"Give us a couple of seconds Lieutenant," replies von Braun.

"I've completed an initial inspection on Engine 6," says Ensign Smith as he appears over the edge of Engine 5, "There are some visible micro fractures on the outside."

"We'll have to wait till we conduct an internal inspection to see if they can be patched," says Kōno moving to the opposite edge.

178

"We've got power patched into the cover motors," reports von Braun.

"We are clear of the cover," says Kōno as she moves behind the engine, "You can open it when ready."

"Beginning opening procedure," notifies von Braun as six motors on the perimeter of the engine hum to life. After a few seconds, the cover lurches off the engine moving it until a gap of 50 centimetres is between the cover and engine before stopping.

"The cover is in holding position," says von Braun.

"We are moving in for a closer inspection," say Kōno as the two spacewalkers begin moving around from the back of the engine. As they reach the engine they begin looking into the engine with their torches.

Inside the engine, pieces of equipment can be seen floating around, damaged by the explosion.

"The cracks on the cover penetrate all the way in," says Smith inspecting the inside of the cover.

"I think that would be 'all the way out' Ensign," corrects Kōno as she begins inspecting the cover, "Some of the magnetic coils are not damaged too bad away from the cracks but the others will be unsalvageable."

The two then turn their attention into the engine. The debris' seem to be small and staying within the engine.

"You can open it up all the way now Lieutenant, we shouldn't have much problem with debris," says Kōno.

"Beginning the second sequence," replies von Braun as the motors come back to life extending the cover further out from the engine. After about 15 minutes the cover extends out one and a half metres and comes to a stop.

"We're going in," says Kōno as she begins to move herself

between the cover and engine sides.

Once the two astronauts are inside they attach an electromagnetic generator to the side of the engine and activate it. The floating debris begins moving to the edges and sticking to the sidewalls.

Once the debris are cleared the two begin inspecting the interior equipment.

"It looks like the lines to the coolant system melted over," say Smith taking photographs to document the inspection, "We should inspect the other side to see if they can be removed and attached to the spare engines."

"It looks like there was a breach in conduit 6 that lead to the explosion," says Kōno inspecting the conduits that lead from the pre-fire inlet to the engine cover. The conduits start from a central distribution section, splitting out into 16 conduits that rest into the inlet ports on the cover.

Kōno floats over to the cover.

"There is also damage to the cover at the same inlet," says Kōno, "Looking at the damage pattern around the inlet port I'd say the breach occurred on the seal between the conduit and port."

"Do you think the seal was damaged by the overload?" asks von Braun.

"It looks like it," replies Kōno, "I'll bring it back in with me to inspect further. Any luck on getting the cover on engine 3 to open."

"Not yet. The damage might have taken out the motor system," says von Braun.

"We'll looking at the damage in here I doubt we'll be using that engine again anyway," says Kōno looking around the

180

engine, "Ensign, I'll get you to take some samples of the searing around conduit 6. I'll begin gathering up the debris."

Inside Engineering, von Braun is inspecting some of the photos as they upload from the cameras.

"Thanks for coming over Lieutenant," says Foley as he floats into the engineering module.

"No worries sir, I did design the engines after all," replies von Braun.

"How's the inspection going?"

"The EVA team have begun their inspection on the inside of engine 5, we might have come up with a cause for the containment failures," says von Braun bringing up the image of the conduit inlet seal, "From what I can tell the seal between a conduit and the cover was breached. Based on some of the test we conducted on Earth when we designed these engine it looks like a high intensity breach of the seal."

"So you think it was the fuel?"

"Not quite sir. The gas breaks down into plasma, which is then repelled away from the engines. What ever this gas is it created significantly more plasma then the engines could handle. There was a failure in Engine 6's transfer conduit close to the pre-fire chamber that caused the internal explosion but the failure occurred in the actual engines for numbers 3 and 5."

"Do you know why they occurred in the engines that are damaged?"

"Best guess is once the first breach occurred the plasma then moved to that side of the ship. Though now that I think about it the station was tethered to that side of the ship."

"Thanks for that Lieutenant. I'm heading back up to the ring now. Send a report up on the other engines once they have been looked at," says Foley.

"Yes sir," says von Braun.

"Kōno to Engineering, I've completed gathering up the debris. I'll need the vacuum from the SEV to mop up the small debris once the electromagnetic generator is offline."

"The SEV should be finished photographing engine 2 in about 5 minutes. I'll have it repositioned once it's finished," replies von Braun.

"We'll continue inspections of the engine here until it's in position," says Kōno.

"How are the engine inspections going over their Captain?" asks Fisher from the station Ops over the radio.

"We've completed the initial inspections on engines 3 through 6 over the past three days," replies Foley, "We are going to have to use two of the four spares and completely replace 3 and 5. We'll also have to inspect all the seals between the plasma conduits and covers on the others before we use them."

"How many spares of those have you got?" asks Fisher.

"About a dozen, they were sent up to be replaced after the shakedown so we could then send some used ones back to Earth to be checked."

"Was it that fuel?"

"Looks like it. The inspection on the breached seals confirms it. There are no weak spots or seams on them as they were carved during manufacturing."

"Are we still looking at a lengthy inspection?"

"I'm afraid so. All we've done at the moment is scanned the exterior of the covers with the SEV and opened the covers on engines 3 through 6. They aren't going to inspect the others until the open ones are reassembled. How's the station going over there?" asks Foley.

"Not good at all. We've confirmed that the ZeroG Core module is fine and we can use it again. We've got power back to Platform 4 and those modules are operating normally," replies Fisher.

"That's good, so we've got the American, Asian and commercial ZeroG Platforms, what about the European modules?" asks Foley.

"We're going to look at them today. The hull breach is in Columbus and we'll do a complete inspection on Cook before opening the hatch to it," says Fisher, "But I've got to tell you Captain, we are mostly dead weight over here."

"How so?"

"There is quite a lot of damage. Equipment has been torn and damaged from quite a lot of the racks around here."

"How much do you think is salvageable Commander?"

"We're going to compile a list for you now though it will take about a week to completely test every piece of equipment," responds Fisher.

"Well we're not going anywhere soon. How are Lenz and Li going in Kibō?" asks Foley.

"They are mounting the force spectrometer on the Exposed Facility as we speak. Once they have completed that they will be able to begin testing what ever that chemical is," says Fisher, "Any idea what it is Captain?"

"Our science lab hasn't been able to directly identify it yet, though it does have a high electron count," replies Foley, "Once the tests are complete send the results over."

"Aye Captain."

"Lieutenant, the test on the force spectrometer is complete and is showing normal," informs Ensign Li.

"Thank you Ensign, move the first sample into place," orders Lieutenant Lenz.

"How are things going down here gentlemen?" asks Fisher floating into Kibō's Pressurised Module.

"We are mounting the first sample now sir," informs Lenz.

"How much are you using in the first test?" asks Fisher.

"One millilitre."

"That little?"

"Only about 2 litres were put through the engines on the Enterprise and look at the damage that caused."

"I suppose you're right Lieutenant," says Fisher.

"The canister is in place," informs Li.

"Ok, excite the liquid," orders Lenz.

The platform on the Exposed Module begins to vibrate causing the liquid to break up into a fine mist inside the canister.

"We are read now sir," says Li.

Lenz looks at Fisher, who gives a reassuring nod.

"Okay, activating the ignition sequence," says Lenz tapping a few buttons on his console.

The vibrations stop on the platform and a door on the canister swivels up and out of the way. As the gas escapes into a second tube it is ignited, causing a paper seal to break opposite to the force spectrometer. As the ignited gas escapes it pushes the canister back onto the spectrometer giving a reading on how much thrust is generated.

"The spectrometer is showing a reading of 3 kilonewtons," reports Li.

"3 kN, from that small amount, what does the normal fuel generate?" asks a surprised Fisher.

"Argon would barely register on this scale sir, maybe 2 or 3 newtons at that level," says Lenz.

"And the plasma that would have been generated?" queries Fisher.

"Probably on the same scale, the engines would have over loaded immediately," speculates Lenz.

"I'll inform the Enterprise. Continue testing to see how it scales up with larger amounts," orders Fisher.

"Have you talked to the Captain yet?" asks Lenz.

"About what Lieutenant?' enquires Fisher.

"About the station sir."

"I think we are both on the same page their Lieutenant."

"Even though this module is almost 30 years old we need something like it on the Enterprise. We don't have an external platform like this."

"I'll see what I can do Lieutenant," assures Fisher.

Chapter Twenty-One – The New Road Home

"Where do you think you are going Lieutenant?" enquires Ross entering the airlock module as Kōno begins suiting up.

"I'm need out there to complete the inspections," replies Kōno.

"The Captain ordered you to have a break today," says Ross.

"He's going to have to come down here and drag me out of this airlock-"

"I know you want to get these inspections over with, but the temper your showing me is why the Captain ordered you to rest for the day."

"As I said-"

"Lieutenant, the Captain isn't going to drag you out of here because he wants to see you," says Ross drilling her point further, "Not here... on the Ring."

"Why?" asks Kōno.

"Because he ordered you to," says Ross putting her hand on Kōno's wrist stopping her from continuing to suit up, "We all want to get moving Lieutenant, but we need to do more than just inspect the engines. We've got to plan how we're getting home."

Kōno stops suiting up and exhales in defeat.

"Here are the latest findings on the fuel. Take a look over them then I'll meet you in the Rotation module to head down," says Ross handing over a tablet and leaving the airlock.

Kōno begins looking over the tablet floating in mid air while removing her suit. Once stowed away she heads out of the airlock back into the core.

Upon arriving in the rotation module Kōno sees Ross getting strapped into an elevator and floats over to the neighbouring seat.

After being strapped in the elevator begins the descent to the ring.

"I've had a look at these findings. That fuel is pretty powerful stuff," says Kōno.

"You're telling me," replies Ross, "We still don't know what it is though."

"The material tests look promising too, I might actually use one of the damaged engines to test whether we can actually use it and in what quantities," says Kōno.

Kōno turns to face Ross who is giving her a weird look.

"It's not that I don't trust the tests being conducted on the station," says Kōno.

"It's not that Lieutenant," says Ross looking just above Kōno's head.

As the gravity begins to take effect Kōno's untied hair begins to settle all over her face and head.

"You see, you're so worn out you didn't even remember to keep your hair tidy," says Ross.

"You're right," says Kōno, searching her pocket for a hair band when Ross hands her one, "These engines are going to take another couple of days to put back together until we can actually start inspecting the undamaged ones. It's already been six days."

"I know Lieutenant, we're all a bit like that by now,"

reassures Ross as the elevator slows and reaches the ring.

As the door opens Lieutenant's Madison and Pirogov assist the two crewmembers.

"I think you're going to like this meeting Commander," says Madison.

"Why's that Lieutenant?" enquires Ross.

"Lieutenant Commander Singh and I made a few interesting discoveries this morning," says Madison.

"Well then, spill the beans," says Ross.

"I think our trip home is going to be more interesting than previously thought, as long as Kōno agrees with out calculations," replies Madison.

"And what are those calculations?" asks Kōno.

"Commander Singh will inform you when you arrive in the conference room," says Madison as she helps Kōno up while Pirogov wheels a chair to the elevator door.

"I do not need that," says Kōno defiantly.

"It's been almost four weeks since you were in gravity Lieutenant," says Pirogov as Kōno steadies herself in the elevator doorframe then begins walking out onto the deck.

"See, I told you," says Kōno before slightly stumbling then regaining her composure.

"Well if you insist, I'll be following right behind you," says Pirogov, "If you make it all the way I'll even leave the chair outside the room."

"So, how are you and Yakov handling the situation," asks Kōno as the crewmembers begin navigating the ring.

"Is that an appropriate question Lieutenant?" responds Pirogov.

"We all knew you two were getting a little friendly on the surface before we left," says Madison.

"And what is wrong with that?" states Pirogov.

"Nothing," says Madison prodding further, "So the two of you are friends?"

"Maybe a little," says Pirogov with a slight smile.

"I knew it," says Kōno over her shoulder, "The first outer space romance."

"I wouldn't quite call it a romance yet," interjects Pirogov.

"Oh no?" responds Madison.

"No," says Pirogov, "We are just two friends. We are the only Russians out here you know. We get along because of our… our heritage."

"So that's what they call it in Russia these days. Heritage," says Madison.

"Yes," says Pirogov confidently, sneaking another smile to Madison, "But we haven't seen much of each other with Yakov over on the station doing the testing."

"I've got a feeling that won't last very long," says Madison as they arrive at the conference room, "I'll be in ops."

"Welcome Ladies," says Foley as the crewmembers enter the conference room. The room takes up one side of a module just under 6 and a half meters long. In the centre of the room is a mahogany desk, one of the few luxuries from Earth on the Enterprise. Three chairs are fixed to the floor on each side, with one at either end.

"Lieutenant Foster, have you got that video link operational yet?" asks Foley into an intercom while the crewmembers take their seats.

"Coming online now sir, patching it through," replies Foster with an image of the station operations module appearing on a display at the opposite end of the table.

"Commander, you there?" says Foley as nobody is on the

screen.

"Give me a moment Captain," replies Fisher as he moves a few panels then rotates the camera.

"That's better," says Foley, "Well then, I'd like to welcome everyone to the first Heads of Staff meeting of the Enterprise. We've got a few things to get through today and I thought it would be better if we we're all involved in the conversations. Kōno, what's the status on the engine inspections?"

"We've completed the inspection and clean-up on engines 3 through 6. We're going to have to replace numbers 3 and 5 with the spares we've got attached to the hull," says Kōno, "The inspections on the seals on the other engines are all clear and we are ready to begin inspecting the other engines when we're ready."

"How's the repair schedule looking?" asks Fisher.

"It will take about 6 hours on each engine to re-seat the seals on the conduits in each engine. The process involves extending the conduits from their normal positions out closer to the cover, then testing to see if any gas escapes through the seals. Once they are seated properly both the conduits and cover are retracted at the same time and a final gas test is conducted to ensure a proper retraction."

"What about the conduits inside lower engineering?" asks Foley.

"They will only take about an hour for each of them. So far it looks like we only need to replace 3, 5 and 6's conduits. But we've only got four spares."

"So that means we've only got one left?" says Foley.

"That's correct, though I may be able to salvage the two intact conduits. I wouldn't push those too hard though," replies Kōno.

"Okay, How's the inspection going over their Commander?" asks Foley turning his attention to the display.

"We haven't lost much equipment over here it's just the electrical distribution systems and lack of energy generation that's the problem," says Fisher, "We've definitely lost Columbus but Cook seems to have popped a seal on the hatch. Once it's closed we'll know if we can still use it again."

"And all the spacecraft we sent over?"

"They are all fine. We've repaired Excalibur and it's operational again," says Fisher, "Though I don't think we will get this ring moving again. We just don't have enough energy on either side for a full rotation restart."

"That's unfortunate Commander. I'll have the SEV sent over to take another look at the truss again to see if we can get some power back through that solar array," says Foley.

"I hope so Captain, otherwise the station will just be a drain on the Enterprise," remarks Fisher.

"Singh, have you been able to figure out what is in the fuel pods yet?" asks Foley.

"Not yet sit, it shares some commonality to its original form in Argon but it's quite complex," says Singh, "We should be able to do a small sample analysis of it while it's burning over on Kibō. That might shed some light onto exactly what it is."

"Could we still use it as a fuel if needed?" asks Foley.

"As long as we limit the flow of ions to the standard tolerances and the heat in the pre-fire chamber doesn't exceed operating guidelines we should be able to use it, just not in such quantities as we did," says Singh, "What's the minimum injection volume rate into the pre-fire chamber?"

"About 50 millilitres per second," replies Kōno.

"I'll run some calculations and tests but I don't think it would be much of a problem," says Singh, "Our 100 millilitre test barely shook the station, though in the engines it might behave differently."

"Pirogov, how's the crew holding up?," Foley asks of his medical officer.

"Quite well under the circumstances, though it's still a hard slog and the crew will be pushing themselves hard for a few weeks yet. If we keep up the rest periods we should be alright," replies Pirogov.

"And the two crew that we're stuck in the stations ZeroG platform," asks Foley.

"They aren't showing any residual signs of decompression sickness," responds Fisher from the station, "They are as alert as they would normally be."

"Excellent, and our food stocks?" enquires Foley.

"The rationing is holding up quite well, though I'd like to start building that hydroponic system we were speculating about. I'm not sure about you guys but I'd like some fresh food to go with these vacuum packed meals," says Pirogov.

"I'll get Madison and Lenz to help you get started with that," says Foley, "So, how well are we travelling?"

"There's no change in speed or course, but Singh and I have been discussing something," says Ross as she moves over to the display behind the Captain, "We've been making some calculations as to what that fuel can achieve for us. If we can get the engines operating within specification we are going to have a very interesting trip."

"How so?" asks Foley.

"We are already going faster than we predicted we would achieve under normal engine operation," says Ross tapping the screen, "But if we can achieve a steady thrust output of half of what we experienced this is what we could be looking at."

As the screen changes to a map of the Gliese 581 star system, an animation begins playing showing the course of the ship moving toward the star. As it get's closer the ship move and Gliese 581d begin to catch up.

"This simulation shows that we would actually pass by several of the planets in the star system, first 581d, then we would use 581g for a gravity assist, putting us 50 degrees off course," says Ross as the animation continues showing the movement of the ship through the system, "Once we meet up with 581c we will be able to correct the course back to Earth using another gravity assist. We will then pass by the star and then intercept 581a before 581c's orbit catches up with us again before departing the star system back to Earth. It's not quite the grand tour Captain but it is achievable."

"Will we intercept any asteroid belt on the way out?" asks Fisher.

"Not as far as we can tell, though any asteroids might still be shielded by the star," says Singh.

"And how soon would be need our engines," enquires Foley.

"That's the good part sir," says an excited Ross, "we wouldn't even need to use the engines for more than 5%

194

of the journey. As long as we start sometime within the next month or so we won't miss out first opportunity."

"That could be achievable Captain," says Kōno, "Looking at these results on the fuel we probably won't even need anymore then two or three engine to achieve that level of acceleration. We could even do repairs to damaged engines on the fly."

"Okay everyone, let's not get ahead of ourselves," says Foley calming his team down, "This is exciting but we need to focus on the here and now. Kōno keep on repairing the engines. Fisher I want an inventory from the station on supplies and everything salvageable and usable over here. Keep analysing that fuel Singh. Is there anything else we need to talk about? No, meeting adjourned."

As the crew begin leaving the conference room, Foley looks at the repeating animation of the ships potential course on the screen.

"Can you believe it Captain?" asks Ross as she moves beside him, "The chance to explore another star system."

"We were designed to explore our own. All the sensor systems are installed, we've even got a few probes that we were going to test during shakedown," says Foley, "It is exciting Ross, very exciting."

"Phase one conduit extension complete," says von Braun over the radio.

"Acknowledged, conduits are in position," says Kōno from inside engine 6, "Activating the heaters on the cover seals."

Each of the seals are designed to enclose around the conduit. While in space, the cold temperatures allow the seal to expand creating a tight seal over the conduits. Each seal is wrapped in a heater ring designed to cause them to contract, making the inside of the seal large enough to fit the conduit inside without any force. During engine ignition, a coolant system extracts the maximum amount of heat away from the conduit sides preventing the seal from coming loose.

"Do you think heat was the cause for the seal breach?" asks Smith.

"Probably. There must have been too much heat generated by the fuel, though when I test one of the damaged engines we'll have a better idea," replies Kōno as the two EVA crew begin testing the size of the seals with a handheld template, "We'll give the heaters another couple of minutes then we should be ready."

"At least this engine didn't sustain any damage," says Smith, "Do you think the conduit failure saved it?"

"Those internal conduits did have a manufacturing problem back on Earth that we picked up during testing," says von Braun, "But they assured us they modified the design to eliminate the problem, at least that's what our tests show."

"That problem was a lateral fracture across the conduit. The one I removed look liked it had a fracture running along the conduit," says Kōno, "I guess we'll find out later."

"These guides are moving in the seals freely now Lieutenant," says Smith moving between the seals.

"I agree they look ready. Prepare for maximum extension

von Braun," says Kōno as she begins to attach a laser guidance system to a couple of the conduits to ensure proper alignment, "We are ready out here."

"The program is ready Lieutenant," informs von Braun.

"Begin."

As the conduits begin moving forward slowly, the EVA crew monitor the lasers as they move closer millimetre by millimetre.

"Adjust one increment clockwise," orders Kōno as the conduits rotate, "That's a good alignment, keep it moving and stop on my mark. Three, Two, One, Mark."

The conduits stop barely touching the insides of the seals.

"Okay, bring it forward for one second," says Kōno as the conduits move forward and seat themselves in the seal, causing a slight shake of the cover.

"Disabling the heaters. Let the seals vent off on their own," says Kōno as the EVA crew shut down the power packs attached to the heaters, "Have you got the gas canister hooked up to the internal conduit yet?"

"Foster has just finished attaching it now and is sealing it off," says von Braun.

"These seals look like they are expanding evenly Lieutenant," says Smith.

"So are these," says Kōno, "Take out your laser measurement tool and check for any gaps in the seal."

The laser imager used the light generated by the laser to check for any minute gaps in any objects it scans. Usually an ultrasound tool would be used however the Enterprise didn't have one in stock.

"The thermal spectrometer is showing the seals are at the same temperature as the conduit," says Smith, "Lasers are showing a good seal as well."

"Okay, detach the heaters and stow them," orders Kōno.

Each heater element is a circular ring broken in the middle with a hinge on one side allowing the ring to swing open and close around a pipe. From one side a wire trails out into a power pack. The power pack attached magnetically to the cover to hold it firmly in place. The heating rings can vary in thickness and heat intensity for a variety of purposes.

"Foster has the gas canister sealed and tested around the conduit," says von Braun, "We are ready in here."

After tying up the cables and stowing them in their EVA bags, the two EVA crew get into position. The lasers have been attached to make any escaping gas more visible.

"We are in position inside the engine," says Kōno, "Is the SEV in position outside."

"It's in position and recording Lieutenant."

Kōno looks to Smith seeing a ready nod.

"Open the canister," says Kōno.

"Canister open and discharging," says von Braun, "We are ready to open the conduit flow valve."

"Do it."

A slight hiss can be heard through the conduits as the gas rushes though to escape into the vacuum of space.

"Do you see any sign of a seal breach Ensign?" asks Kōno.

"Not that I can see," says Smith as he studies the seals on his half of the cover.

"Canister depleted," says von Braun as the rushing gas stops.

"How did the SEV look?' asks Kōno.

"It looks like an even distribution out all the emitters,"

says von Braun.

"Okay, let's gather up our things and we will re-seat the cover and conduct another test," says Kōno.

"Sounds good Lieutenant," says von Braun.

"When your done von Braun I want you to take the smaller piece of engine 3 over with you. It still has a complete seal and emitter. Hook it up to Kibō and test it at the minimum flow rate. I want to make sure it can handle what we are throwing at it."

"Will do that. I think Foster and Li have the hang of it so I won't be needed over here much longer," replies von Braun.

From the outside the transfer pod looks like any other module. A 6 metre diameter cylinder and 6 metres long, the primary purpose is to transfer people and equipment between the station and ship. Each side of the pod has a standard docking hatch, though made more resilient than a normal hatch due to frequent use. The interior has 8 standard rack slots along each side of the module for storage, with a controller's station at each end next to the hatch to control the speed of the pod. Unlike in normal operations where the tether is taught and straight, the tether is currently loose due to the close proximity of the ship and station. This also requires the manoeuvring systems to be utilised to ensure proper orientation of the pod for docking, and to ensure the pod doesn't begin taking up any of the slack on the tether, which could cause damage to the connections on either side.

"We should connect the two Russian platforms together," says Foley as Kōno navigates the pod toward the station, "If we keep on using this pod it will take forever to just move personnel around."

"Are you going to keep the station attached?" enquires Kōno.

"After what happened a few days ago I don't think there is any way," replies Foley looking over a tablet, "With the Ring's rotation shut down and no power systems beyond the generators it's going to be difficult."

"I was just thinking the same thing Captain," says Kōno as she begins to manoeuvre the pod for docking on the station.

As the pod begins approaching the dock on the station, Kōno observes Fisher already waiting for their arrival. After a few minutes to allow the space between the two dock's hatches to equalise the pressure, Kōno opens the hatch.

"It's good to have to back Lieutenant," says Fisher, "There are a few systems I want you to check on the wing."

"I'll get right to it sir," says Kōno as she floats past.

"So how are things over here Commander?" asks Foley as he floats through the hatch.

"Captain, I didn't know you were coming over," says Fisher knocked off guard.

"Well we've got a few things to discuss," says Foley, "Besides, I've had enough of the comm system and I wanted to see this place myself."

"Well then follow me Captain," says Fisher as he floats up the core, "Things are not great over here at all. We've only got enough power to keep the lights on, a few sensors and

200

computers."

"It does look a bit dark over here," comments Foley as he stops to inspect the same buckled bulkhead that Fisher first spotted upon his arrival.

"Don't worry about that Captain, it's a smooth buckle. No cracks, fractures or weak areas," says Fisher continuing up the core, "I don't know if it was those engines or a combination of that and what brought us here but the electrical system has had it."

"In what way?"

"Most of the equipment is fine, it just looks like the circuit breakers overloaded and damaged the distribution grid. The reserve grid is fine as it was designed to take everything that could be thrown at it, but apart from the essentials everything from the Core out to the Ring is shot. The ZeroG platform is fine though."

"How's that inventory going that I asked for?"

"As I said the essential systems like life support and environments systems still work. We've tested the medical bay and it looks good. So do the water and oxygen recyclers so we can still use those."

"And the ZeroG platform?"

"It was only the Euro platform that took damage since that is where the stress was located," says Fisher, showing a bit of regret being from Europe himself, "Being old Columbus took the brunt of the damage and breached but Cook seams fine, your guys have confirmed the hatch is still good. All the spacecraft are fine as well. We can begin transferring some back over to Enterprise."

"I think we'll have to transfer all of them," says Foley.

"So I suppose you are thinking what I'm thinking?"

enquires Fisher.

"What's that Commander?" challenges Foley.

"Let's get rid of the station," says Fisher, "I think she is too badly damages. Even if we remained attached she would just be a drain on your systems and supplies."

"That's what I was thinking," admits Foley.

"It's not like you don't have enough space over there. You were designed to hold up to 100 people."

"There are only twenty of us out here now."

"Twenty, can we operate the Enterprise with that small a crew?"

"Well our shakedown crew was going to be twenty, we'll just have to be careful with crew rotations between the Ring and Core to ensure nobody spends too much time in zero gravity," says Foley, "It's going to take some tricky planning but I think we can do it."

"Do you want me to start a list of equipment we can take over to Enterprise?" asks Fisher.

"That will be great Commander," says Foley, "But don't forget we've only got four empty storage modules over there."

"Well with some of the ZeroG modules we should be able expand that to six," replies Fisher.

"I'll order a reorientation of the station and connect the Russian modules together to assist in the transfer once we get the tether untangled," says Foley, "And don't forget to add some piping or conduits to the list, we need it for the hydroponic system the science staff are designing. We might even have to break into the Seed Vault to diversify our food stocks."

"That shouldn't be a problem, as long as we have a sealed

chamber to provide clean access," says Fisher in agreement, "I got that updated flight plan from Singh, he thinks once we clear Gliese 581 we should be able to punch the engines up and get home in about 80 years,"

"It is promising," says Foley, "But I don't think any of us will get home to Earth."

"But the ship will Captain," says Fisher adding with a bit of cheek, "And maybe Ensign Li."

Chapter Twenty-Two – Final Transfers

"Docking is complete Captain," notifies Ross after the no ops period passes without incident.

"Very good commander, notify the station to pressurise the hatch and we'll begin equipment transfers ASAP," says Foley, "Are you ready to begin transferring the ZeroG modules from the station Shipway?"

"Yes sir, we're just waiting for the all clear then we'll begin undocking and passing across the modules to the Enterprise within the hour," says Shipway, "I'm just about to head down now to supervise from the core."

"Station is reporting the ZeroG modules are full and ready to be detached," informs Foster.

"Well then Shipway you better get down there," says Foley as Shipway leaves his console and heads toward an elevator.

The atmosphere aboard the ship and station has been upbeat for the last few days. The inspections on the other engines have come back clear and their reassembly has gone off without a hitch. All of the equipment that is being salvaged has been secured within the three ZeroG platforms to be moved across to the Enterprise. Since the engine problems just over 9 days ago the progress that has been made by the crew has impressed Captain Foley.

As Shipway arrives at the ZeroG platform, the first of the supplies being transferred through the Russian modules are being passed through to be stored in the existing storage module.

"It's a good thing you Russians installed a viewing port

outside this module or we'd be bumping our toes every few seconds," says Shipway as he arrives ready to conduct the module transfers between the station and ship.

"I've moved Arm 2 into position here ready to grapple the Asian platform as it is handed over," says Lenz, "Kibō has already been detached and is being held onto by it's own arm ready for separate installation."

"Very good Lieutenant," admires Shipway.

"I'll be controlling the station arm from these consoles, you can use those consoles to operate the ships arms," says Lenz.

"It's a good thing we only need to move two platforms, otherwise this could have taken a couple of days."

"Yes, it is thoughtful of the Captain to leave Cook attached then dock the Russian platform together."

"I thought about keeping Cook attached," corrects Shipway, "The Captain though docking this platform together would be quicker for transfers."

"Yes, that pod can be slow at times," agrees Lenz.

"Jackson to Enterprise, the Asian platform is heading your way. It will be ready for hand over in a few minutes," says Jackson from the station.

"Thank you station, I'm manoeuvring the arm into place now," replies Lenz as the arm begins moving along the rail on the module.

The rail system was added to ensure the arms weren't required to move 'hand over hand' around the spacecraft. This allowed for a shorter but more flexible arm that only needed to hand off to another arm when moving between the Core and ZeroG platforms.

"We are in place on this side station," informs Lenz as the

Asian platform begins rotating away from the station. The new 'Zhishi' Chinese module is attached directly to the ZeroG platform, with the Kibō modules having been recycled from the first International Space Station. As the modules move away from the station, they perform a graceful pirouette, manoeuvring the modules so the Kibō grapple fixture on the Experiment Logistics Module faces the effector on the arm on the Russian platform. Once in position, the arm on the station moves the platform toward the arm, keeping the alignment pin oriented to the effector on the arm. Once the pin enters the effector, it is secured by a mechanism wrapping around the pin and several secondary magnets help secure the grapple to the arm.

"Platform grappled and secured," announces Lenz over the radio.

"Detaching the arm over here," replies Jackson as the arm on the station begins retreating from the Chinese module.

"The station arm is at the safe distance," says Jackson.

"Beginning manoeuvres on the platform." replies Lenz as the Russian arm begins to pivot and rotate the modules so the Enterprises arm will be able to grip the Chinese module, ready for installation. Once the manoeuvre is complete, the platform begins moving toward the ship. The two operators have an excellent view from the platform designed to mimic the original Cupola module on the original ISS.

During the time it takes for the arm to traverse the remainder of the station's Russian modules, Shipway manoeuvres the Enterprises arm into position ready to accept the transfer.

"Okay, the platform is in position," says Lenz with the Asian ZeroG platform looming large over the observation platforms windows.

"Moving the arm under the grapple fixture," says Shipway watching the consoles. While the view is impressive, the precision required is beyond even the sharpest eye on the Enterprise, "Okay, the effector is aligned. Beginning grapple."

"Solar array retraction is confirmed," says Madison from the starboard truss of the station, "I'm latching the cover."

"Copy that," says Foster from the SEV. Unlike its earlier configuration, the standard on-orbit module is now attached to the bottom of the SEV to allow for more external storage space.

As Madison latches the cover over the solar array, Foster swings the SEV around so the rear is facing the truss. The radiator from the same side has already been removed and strapped down on the rear platform of the SEV.

"The cover is latched," says Madison, "I'm going to begin disconnecting the motor box."

Once the motor has been disconnected, the panel only requires a few bolts to be removed to detach it from the truss. Madison reaches into her toolbox to retrieve the electric spanner.

"I never thought I'd be pulling this place apart piece by piece," says Madison.

"I don't think anybody did Lieutenant," replies Foster, "Make sure you secure those bolts, we don't need to lose any of them out here."

"I did bring the magnetic plate Lieutenant," says Madison, "I just wish I completed that SEV operations course before I came up here. You know in the old days everyone had to do pretty much well everything before they would let us go up."

"Yeah, but in those days it took years just to plan and train for a single routine mission," says Foster, "I don't have any problems being prepared for any situation, but everyone had to know how to fly a space shuttle even if it wasn't their job."

"Okay, I've got the final bolt secured and the assembly is moving freely," informs Madison.

"Stand-by while I back this thing up," says Foster as she moves the SEV closer to the truss.

"You're getting close," says Madison counting down the distance, "Three, two, one, mark."

With a slight puff of gas the SEV becomes stationary with about 15 centimetres between it and the truss.

"Begin securing the assembly Lieutenant," says Foster, "and don't forget you've got to get back on there to get back in."

"We should have removed the solar canopy before we started," says Madison.

To increase energy generation, the solar canopy was installed on the SEV. The canopy covers the rear deck doubling as a light shade and radiation shield.

Once Madison secures the assembly to the platform she gathers up the two toolboxes she was using on the truss then reattaches her suit to the suitport. After a few seconds to allow air to be released into the area between the door and the suit, Foster moves over to the suitport and opens the door.

"I still hate these things," says Madison as the door is opened, "and now for the difficult part."

People think getting out of these suits would be easy, but with the lack of gravity the arms and legs are a bit too flexible making the job of untangling oneself from the suit much more difficult. Think of it like trying to take two jumpers and a shirt off while trying to keep another shirt on underneath at the same time.

"I still think they should have installed magnetic latches to secure the arms," says the extracted Madison, "And now I've got to wear a jumpsuit over this sweatsuit. Too many suits."

"Don't worry. We'll be back on the Enterprise in a few minutes," chuckles Foster at her crewmates frustration as she returns to the controls, "Then you can get a fresh change of clothes."

The SEV begins traversing the distance between the stations truss and the docking port on the Enterprise above the ZeroG platform.

"Looks like they are turning the lights out," comments Madison as she joins her crewmate at the front of the SEV.

"Yep, it won't be long now."

Chapter Twenty-Three – The Final Goodbye

The station now sits dark in space. A bit lighter than when it arrived, the systems have been shut down in almost all modules. The internal lights have been switched off in all the modules except the ZeroG central platform and the Core storage module above it.

"We're ready to extend the solar arrays Commander," says von Braun.

As one of the first modules launched, the storage module just above the ZeroG platform contains it's own solar panels and communications systems.

"Roll them out Lieutenant," says an exhausted Fisher.

On opposite sides of the modules the solar arrays deploy. Much smaller than their larger cousins, they provided enough power to keep four modules running before the first sections of the truss arrived two months later during construction.

"It's a good idea to do this Commander," says Foley, the three being the last crewmembers on the station.

"It will allow us, and future generations to track the station," says Fisher, "This module is the most protected on the station. They said it would last for a century before being abandoned. Lets hope it does."

"Arrays are extended," informs von Braun, "They are generating enough energy for the transmitter sir."

"Very well Lieutenant. Let's go," says Fisher.

As the three begin moving down into the ZeroG platform, Fisher begins reminiscing about the time spent aboard the station. Stopping in the platform, Fisher gives the station one final look then follows von Braun and Foley through the hatch closing the station side behind him.

"Well that's it," says Fisher to the four surviving station crew waiting in the ship module, "I hope no one left the oven on."

Foley then leads the crew back into the ship and up into the core. Arriving in a habitat module, the entire ships crew is waiting for the moment.

"You know, final goodbyes are always the hardest," says Fisher, "As I can attest this has been one of the hardest decisions any commanding officer can make. We tried everything to keep her but in the end it just wasn't meant to be. This time we've made the right choice for the good of the ship and the good of our new mission. She provided humanity with its first sample of artificial gravity in space and inspired this ship and it's mission. It showed us that we could not only generate gravity in space, but that gravity could alleviate the ills our body feel from the lack of gravity. It proved that we could spend years in space and still have the capability to stand on our own two feet when we got back to Earth. We should also not forget those that won't get the chance to head back to Earth with us. Their sacrifice reminds us that what we do here is dangerous, and we need to respect not only our own limits, but our spacecraft's limits."

"To our fallen crew," toasts Foley.

"Hear here," reply the crew.

"And to the station, farewell old friend," toasts Fisher with a tear in his eye.

"Hear here."

212

"Crew to attention," orders Foley.

After a moments silence Fisher looks toward Foley whom nods in approval.

"Release," orders Fisher as von Braun taps a button on a console.

Outside the station a flash of gas can be seen as the hatch decompresses and the station begins moving away from the Enterprise. The computer on-board the station then activates the tracking beacon, which is played on the ship's intercom. The RSC system on the station sets the station rotating and provides a further push away from the Enterprise.

"Crew, Dismissed!" orders Foley.

Fisher remains at the viewing window watching his station float away from the Enterprise.

"Don't worry about her Commander," reassures Foley, "She'll do just fine."

"How are those sensors going?" asks Kōno.

"Engine 2 is online Lieutenant," responds Madison.

"Brining Engine 6's online now," responds Shipway.

To ensure safe operations with the new fuel, Kōno has ordered additional sensors to be installed on the outside of the conduits to detect and hot spots or deformations.

"Are you getting the hang of things Lieutenant?" asks Kōno.

"I think so," says von Braun, "I'm still getting used to the engines systems on top of everything else."

"Well after this test you'll be about as familiar with them as

I am," says Kōno, "You did help design them."

"That I did," agrees von Braun.

"All done," says Shipway from lower engineering.

"Okay, I want everyone out of there for this test," orders Kōno, "We still don't know if this will work and I don't want to lose anyone else."

The two astronauts in lower engineering gather their tools and exit the module. Once clear, Kōno activates the close sequence on the containment doors, closing several seconds later. Unlike an emergency closure the doors aren't locked but do maintain a full separation between the two modules.

"I'm getting a good connection to the sensors Lieutenant," says von Braun.

"Engineering to Ops, we are ready for the engine tests down here," informs Kōno.

"Thank you Lieutenant," responds Foley as he begins a ship wide broadcast ordering a lockdown in case the test doesn't go as planned.

"Engineering, you have a go for the tests," reports Foley from Ops.

"Okay, here we go. This first test will be incremental on engine 2 to ensure no one stage causes any instability in this new fuel, then the second engine will be on the automated sequence," informs Kōno.

Once everyone is at their stations Kōno begins the manual fire sequence.

"Activate heaters on engine systems," orders Kōno as the crew bring the components up to a usable temperature.

"Pump ready," informs Madison.

"Pre-fire chamber at temperature," says Shipway.

"Conduits are ready," says von Braun.

"Engine at operating temperature," says Kōno, "Activate the pump for 10 millilitres."

"Pump active, sensors detect 10 millilitre. Pump offline," informs Madison.

"Chamber holding the fuel normally and magnetic containment is stable," informs Shipway.

"Open valves and activate magnetic fields," orders Kōno.

"Fields active on the conduits and valves open," replies von Braun.

"Emitters active as well. Okay here we go, watch your sensors," says Kōno preparing herself while activating the intercom, "Engine ignition in five, four, three, two, one, ignite."

"Ignition," reports Shipway as the ship lurches forward for a brief second then stabilises.

"Sensors stable," says von Braun monitoring several consoles.

"Plasma output nominal, registering 20% of rated normal," says Kōno, "All equipment is registering normal. Looks like a good test."

"I'd say that went pretty well," says von Braun, "Containment confirmed across the entire chain. Do you think there are any problems with an automated test?"

"Looks good across the board," says Kōno, "Return the systems on engine 2 to automatic then switch to engine 6. Engineering to Ops, we've had a successful manual test on engine 2 and we're moving to an automated test of engine 6."

"You are going to conduct a test of the automated systems on 2 aren't you?" asks Foley.

"We'll do that when we conduct the sync check Captain," replies Kōno.

"Very well Lieutenant," says Foley.

"Systems on engine 6 are active and ready for the test," informs von Braun.

"I think I might let you do the test Lieutenant," says Kōno.

"Me?"

"Sure, you are the Engineering Chief down here in the core section," says Kōno, "Now's a good a time to start as any."

"Sure thing," replies von Braun swapping consoles with Kōno, "Okay. Activate the pre-flight sequence on engine 6.

"Pre-flight sequence initiating," replies Kōno, "Heaters active, magnetic fields aligned and stable, temperatures are stable."

"Okay, set fuel flow rate to 5 millilitres per second for a four second burst," orders von Braun.

"Injectors set," informs Madison.

"All systems ready," says von Braun activating the intercom, "Activate engines in five, four, three, two, one, ignite."

The ship once again lurches forward.

"All engine systems stable," informs Kōno, "Flow rate at 5 millilitres."

After the four second burst the ship stops its acceleration.

"How are the emitters and seals?" asks von Braun.

"They look stable, no breach and acceleration as expected," replies Kōno.

"Engineering to Ops, the test on the engines is complete.

No problems to report," informs von Braun.

"Good job Lieutenant," says Foley.

Kōno floats over to von Braun to relieve her.

"We are ready to conduct the synchronisation check Captain," says Kōno, "We will start with the minimum injection rate just like the last test and double it over a 10 second burst."

"We are ready when you are," says Foley.

"Return systems to normal," says Kōno.

"Engine systems are back to normal operations," says von Braun exiting the testing mode the engines systems have been in.

"Select Engines 2 and 6 for operations, flow rate starting at 5 millilitres then increasing 1 millilitre every 2 seconds," orders Kōno.

"Engines 2 and 6 active," informs Madison.

"Flow rate programmed and ready," says Shipway.

"Beginning pre-fire sequence," says von Braun, continuing a few seconds late, "Pre-fire sequence complete."

"Engines programmed and ready Captain," says Kōno into the intercom.

"Engage," orders Foley.

"Activating the engines," says Kōno as the ship begins moving once again.

"Magnetic fields stable," reports von Braun, "The plasma stream is being split 49/51."

"That's good enough, the emitters have adjusted to compensate," says Kōno.

While an even split in the stream is desirable, an imbalance of 5% across all engines is acceptable with the emitters redirecting the plasma stream to compensate any extra motion to one side or the other while maintaining enough steering capacity.

"We've got a constant increase from the pump to the prefire chamber," informs Shipway.

"Acceleration is smooth," notes Madison.

"Deactivate engines in three, two, one, mark," orders Kōno.

"Engines offline," informs von Braun, "Fuel flow, ion flow, magnetic emitters are all reporting stable," says von Braun, "No sign of any breach in the engine seals."

"Engineering to Ops, engine test complete," informs Kōno, "Looks like we can handle that new fuel."

"Good work Lieutenant," replies Foley, "All hands stand down from engine tests."

Chapter Twenty-Four – A New Beginning

"Welcome back to the Ring Lieutenant," greats Captain Foley as Kōno enters the ready room.

"Thank you sir," replies Kōno, "I hope I don't get too used to it though."

"We'll be rotating you and Lieutenant von Braun between the Core and the Ring every 28 days as part of the standard crew rotation," says Fisher as the Captain invites Kōno to take a seat on the lounge next to Lieutenant Commander Singh.

"So the tests went well?" asks Foley

"Yes sir," says Kōno handing over a tablet, "The test are inline with the experiments conducted on the damaged engine section as well as the fuel test earlier."

"So the engines can handle the fuel?" asks Fisher.

"Well technically it's the pre-fire chamber that can handle the fuel as that's where it's combusted," says Kōno, "The conduits held up pretty good though I do want to conduct a close-up inspection of the seals on one of the engines once we are under way."

"Why's that Lieutenant?" enquires Foley.

"One of the cameras picked up a slight temperature increase in one of the seals on engine 6 at the start of the sync test," says Kōno, "However it did stabilise after about a second and didn't show any signs of getting worse."

"Could this be a problem?" asks Fisher.

"The computer did increase the flow rate to the coolant pipe around that seal which stabilised it," says Kōno, "But if it was going to become a problem it would have happened during the test. That's when these sorts of things fail. But we can monitor it next time we use the engine and divert the plasma flow to the other emitters on that engine if necessary."

"There does seem to be one piece of great new here,' says Fisher handing the tablet over to Singh, "It looks like the acceleration rate is within specifications."

"Definitely," replies Kōno, "Though I will slow down the increase in fuel injection. The sensors in the pre-fire chambers show a bit of stress during the test. A reduction in the rate will give it some time to cool off, though I wouldn't recommend going any higher than 5 millilitres for each increment."

"These results are in line with the course I've plotted," says Singh, "as long as we can achieve 450 kilometres per second in about a week we should be able to intercept Gliese 581d in two months."

"Yeah we should be able to achieve that in about a week," says Kōno.

"450 kilometres per second," laughs Fisher, "I can't believe we're talking on that scale now."

"Well the engines have taken us up to 4.5 in less than ten seconds, though there were a few explosions," says Kōno.

Fisher looks at the Captain.

"Yeah I can't quite believe it too," expresses Foley, "A month ago I was getting ready to take this ship out for a loop and back and you we're a space station commander. Set the course Commander. We will leave at 0900 in the morning. Let's get some sleep and be well rested."

"Good morning Lieutenant, get a good sleep?" asks Fisher as Lieutenant Foster enters Ops.

"About as good as someone that can't wait for a big day," says Fisher as she takes the navigators station.

"I didn't sleep very well last night either," says Lieutenant Commander Ross entering Ops joining Singh at her neighbouring console.

"If you don't have an objections Lieutenant, let's give the Captain a warm welcome and have this ship pointed in the right direction when he arrives," suggests Fisher.

"RSC systems are ready sir," informs Kōno.

"Set the course Foster," orders Fisher.

"Yes sir," says Foster as she activates the orientation program.

The Enterprise begins rotating away from the Gliese 581 star about 20 degrees anti-orbit before coming to a stop.

"You're a bit eager to get underway Commander," says Foley entering ops from his ready room.

"Just giving you a few extra minutes," replies Fisher standing up from the Captains chair with Foley replacing him.

"Kōno, how are the engines?" asks Foley.

"Ready for the pre-fire sequence sir," reports Kōno.

"Course set Lieutenant?"

"Course laid in and ready Captain," replies Foster.

"How's the crew Commander?"

"The crew is ready and the ship is locked down for acceleration," replies Fisher.

"Well then, I suppose the only thing left for me to do is that speech," say Foley initiating a ship wide broadcast,

"Like many of you I spent a long restless night last night in anticipation for this moment. While I know each and every one of you will continue to perform like you have over the past month, let us not forget those who have sacrificed their lives getting us here. We push forward with this ships mission not for us to get home, but to honour their spirit, dedication and memory. This ship was build for a purpose, exploration and discovery. And while I'll refrain from repeating our historical namesakes' missions, we shall carry them out with every duty we perform. We'll explore these worlds before us and move headstrong into the unknown, broadening our knowledge and horizons on our way to our ultimate goal, home. Let's show the universe our endeavouring human spirit for exploration. Let's Go."

"We're ready Captain," assures Fisher.

"Engage." orders Foley.

With the order the ship's engines light up, carrying it's most precious cargo on its new mission. Exploration, Discovery and nor Lifeboat. As her acceleration increases, a sense of relief sets over her crew. Coasting at speeds they never thought possible, the ship begins its long journey home.

Earth Space Ship Enterprise.

Course Earth.

The Enterprise and her crew will return in:

E.S.S. Enterprise - Into The Unknown

EPILOGUE

CORONAL MASS EJECTION POST-IMPACT MEDIA
BRIEFING   3
UNITED   NATIONS   OFFICE   AT   GENEVA,
SWITZERLAND
14:00 UTC JUNE 29, 2044

"Thank you for attending today. I'm Adilah Ikramm, Director General of the United Nations Office here in Geneva. We are here today to provide an updated briefing on the coronal mass ejection impact and the resulting effects it is continuing to have around the planet. I have with me today the Chief of the Office of Outer Space Affairs committee Rudolf Wenzel and Mark Bridges, Earth Space Centre Deputy Chief Director. I'll let Rudolf speak first."

"Thank you Adilah," says Rudolf, "It's has been a long four days since the impact of the coronal mass ejection and the resulting effects are continuing to be felt around the planet. We can confirm that the strength of the event at peak intensity was greater than that which was felt during the Carrington Event that occurred during the 19th century. The impact started while the European and African continents were facing the sun and ended while the American continents were sunward. As it is summer in the northern hemisphere that is where we have seen the most severe consequences. The energy distribution grids across the European and North American continents remain affected though they are beginning to be restored at a local level starting around power generation facilities moving outward. The loss of equipment has been greatest in North America where only a smaller percentage of the population followed warnings that they need to remove their electronic devices from power grids and disconnect batteries. Of the basic services Hospital and Military assets have received the least amount of damage. Hospitals followed the warnings we gave combined with a level of protection built in to electronic circuitry in medical devices they remained mostly undamaged. Quite a lot of military assets due to their inherit design were protected from the CME. The most affected civilian assets beyond the power grids include the hard lined telephone networks and traffic signalling. I'll pass you back to Adilah for more information."

"Thank you Rudolf," says Adilah, "The civil affects have been far reaching. We are continuing to advise nations to maintain a civil law and order, ensure the local populations are protected and the basics are provided for. There have been no reports of any military movements beyond their national borders or any major civil unrest. So far Australia, New Zealand, most Pacific nations and South East Asian nations remain relatively unaffected by the impact as they were facing away from the main impact areas. Those nations are rushing to provide protective storage for perishable items like foods and medicine stocks. Due to their design most aircraft were able to land at airports around the world without any damage or loss of life however some small and light aircraft wreckage has been found around the world. What will be affected for some time to come will be national economies. Industries like food processing and transportation will be severely affected. As the financial systems around the world rely upon electronic communication it will be almost impossible for years to come to bring those systems back online. While we are not advocating nationalisation of businesses, facilities or industries, we strongly advice governments to provide the necessary assistance to ensure the most essential industries continue to operate and move to restore financial systems where possible. We are also advising governments to take stock of their capacity to create basic necessities like foods and medicines and cooperate with their neighbours where shortfalls occur and to ensure an appropriate rationing of supplies occurs. On an individual level, we are encouraging people who have the space to create food gardens on their properties to ensure a local food supply. Further to this we also encourage smart energy consumption where those individuals have access to energy generators like solar and wind power. We ask these people to only use their energy for food storage and essential communications. During this time people don't need their computers or televisions or even vacuum cleaners so a smart consumption of energy will go a long way. Individuals also need to remember that supplies they previously used will be scarce. Not only electricity, but also supplies like water and petrol will be difficult to obtain and transport over the next few years. If you have any of these supplies use them sparsely. The fuel in your motor vehicle may be all you have access to for weeks or even months. Many communities are going to need to go back to basic items like buckets, bikes and even horses and carriages to survive. If you have these items used them and conserve other supplies. We haven't quite gone back to the dark ages. We have many facilities like roads, hospitals, wireless communications that we can still take advantage of so I say to the people of this planet don't despair. It will be a tough few years, lets hope we can learn from them and emerge a stronger planet with a new human spirit of cooperation. I'll now pass you on to Mark for an update on solar activity and space assets."

"Thanks Adilah," says Mark, "While the next few year will certainly be tough for humanity and this planet we too hope that the human spirit will shine through and we will emerge a much better species. Solar activity has calmed down over the past few days and we currently don't expect any for ejections to threaten Earth. We have seen about 60% of satellites in the path of the CME either go offline or not wake up from the sleep that was designed to help protect them from the CME. We have a limited number of communication satellites active with most being utilised by governments for communications. Most of the weather and observation satellites were able to survive as they maintain a lower orbit and had greater protection from Earths magnetic field. The planets magnetic field is beginning to restore itself to its previous protection levels and aurora activity should return to seasonal norms over the next couple of days. We are using a lot of military communication assets to communicate with satellites and spacecraft and can confirm that the Lunar Observatory space station and the two expeditions on the moons

d

surface are safe with little effect as its orbit around the Earth shielded the moon. However the news on the International Space Station and E.S.S. Enterprise is still not good. We still have no communications contact or any visual observations of either craft. We know from final transmissions around the height of the CME impact that the station was having trouble keeping its Magnetic Shield active however the CME became to intense to maintain radio communications. The last communications we receives from Enterprise was that the station was having problems but their shield was active and protecting the ship. Radar scans of the orbit and surrounding areas are showing there is no debris and there were no reports of any atmospheric re-entry. The station and ship were over Europe at the time and there would have been reports on the ground as many people were observing the aurora across the entire continent. The reports of no debris are of concern as not only is there not station or ship, but no debris what so ever. There is no space junk in a corridor around Earths orbit where there previously was. That could not have been caused by a physical object like an asteroid or meteor as such an object would have been detected and the debris would have been moved around and added to other areas in orbit and we aren't seeing that in our scans. However I do have some good news in the last hour from Australia. They have retrieved a space capsule from the Gibson Desert in Western Australia that was connected to the space station. There are two crewmembers that were found alive in the capsule and they are being treated in hospital. The crewmembers are Lieutenant Antonio Doria of the Italian Space Agency assigned to the Enterprise and Ensign Megan Young a private pilot from the United States company SpaceX assigned to the station. They are both cooperating with authorities and are providing information to CSIRO space division personnel. We don't have any specific information yet but the discovery of this capsule provides us hope that there may be more survivors yet. We are asking governments around the planet to search for the emergency beacons on the specific radio frequencies. That's all from us now and we will provide additional information when it becomes available."

"Thank you Mark. That wraps up this update from the United Nations. A quick update on the situation at UN Headquarters in New York," says Adilah, "We have been able to restore power to most of the essential communication systems that allow us to communicate between governments and local ambassadors can now communicate directly back to their governments. This was previously being relayed through military communication networks provided by the United States military. We hope that we will be able to restore power to other areas the UN headquarters for the next briefing but if not I will see you back here in 6 hours for the next briefing which will include a question and answer session. Thanks for attending."

f

GLOSSARY

$$R = \frac{9.81g}{\left(\frac{\pi \times \text{rpm}}{30}\right)^2}$$

h

To find out more about the author visit

www.rankin.co

www.twitter.com/nicrankin

www.facebook.com/nicrankin.author

To buy or download more books in the Enterprise Series
visit

www.rankin.co/books

or search for "Nic Rankin" at your favourite eBook store.

This book was self-published by the author including
editing and formatting. If you find any writing errors in
this book please contact the author so the next edition can
be improved.